"Just because she's dead doesn't mean you can forget the things she did, Dan."

"Things? What things? Come on, Thyra, level with me!" he shouted.

"Oh—going around with that guy in the Triumph. A big guy. Handsome. At least your wife thought so."

"You're a liar!" he cried hoarsely.

Thyra moved closer. Now her thighs and belly touched him gently, excitingly. "Am I?" she whispered.

"She was my wife."

"Being a wife doesn't make a woman good. She's born good or bad. Like me . . ."

THE BORGIA BLADE
MADAME BUCCANEER
ONE SWORD FOR LOVE
THE GENTLEMAN ROGUE
WOMAN OF KALI
REBEL WENCH
QUEEN OF SHEBA
TERROR OVER LONDON
WITNESS THIS WOMAN

One Wife's Ways

by Gardner F. Fox

WILDSIDE PRESS

One Wife's Ways

CHAPTER ONE

That man tried to kill me!
Dan Kinnick took his shaking hands from the wheel
of his Oldsmobile hardtop and stared after the big Cadillac that had come hurtling out of the darkness with no
lights showing. A man had leaned from the rightside
window with a pistol in his hand and fired it.
At me! He fired at me!
Kinnick felt nausea churn inside him, watching the
red taillights come on as the car roared off into the
night. With a sickly terror, he turned his head to stare
at the bullethole in the closed window at his right.
Cracks stippled the glass in a crazy quilt pattern.
He only missed by an inch! I even felt the bullet. I
felt it go past my chin! Just a little this side, and I
wouldn't have a face. I wouldn't need a face. I'd be
dead!
Kinnick bit his lip and balled his hands into fists and
beat them against the steering wheel. He wanted to
scream, to yell insanely. Things like this didn't happen
to a guy, not in real life. In the movies, sure. You sat
back and watched some poor slob running from a gang
that was out to get him all the time you knew he was
going to get away, no matter how bad the odds. Nobody kills a hero. Dan Kinnick was no hero, though. Nobody was dollying in on him with a movie camera.
He was sitting in a 1962 hardtop, half in and half out
of a ditch along Colonial Road in a residential section
of north Yonkers. There was a bullethole in the suicide
seat window, and he was scared witless.
"A mistake," he mumbled. "It was a mistake. God, it's

7

got to be a mistake. Somebody thought I was another joe. Sure, that must be it."

Only it was no mistake.

Too many queer things had been happening to Dan Kinnick lately for it to be a mistake. Somebody was out to get him, to put him in a coffin six feet under. But why?

He tried to think, but thinking was impossible. All he could do was summon up a chance memory, here and there. His name was Daniel Philip Kinnick. He owned a gas station on Yonkers Avenue. He was almost thirty years old. To his knowledge, he hadn't an enemy in the world.

"I don't know anything that would get anybody in trouble. I don't fool around with somebody's wife. I keep my nose clean. What other reason would there be to kill a guy? I don't know any mobsters. I was never in a racket—"

After a while he realized he was sitting hunched over the wheel, mumbling senselessly to himself. He straightened up and leaned back, shaking his head, taking deep gulps of air in an effort to lessen the sickness in his belly.

He opened the door, got out and walked around the car three times. The crisp December night settled the churning restlessness of his guts. He leaned his hip against a fender and closed his eyes.

Ben Vardon. He was the man to see.

Detective-Sergeant Vardon of the Yonkers Police Department was his friend. If anyone would know why one man killed another, he would.

The hardtop had stalled. It took him a little while to compose himself enough to start the motor and back up onto the roadway. The sickness was still in him and he had to take a solid grip on himself. Then, he thought, suppose they're waiting for me up ahead to make another try? The sickness came back so bad he opened the car door and stepped out again, nausea in his guts, until his nerves quieted down.

He drove a mile without lights, almost wishing a patrol car would flag him down and give him a ticket. At least they wouldn't shoot him and he'd have somebody to tell his story to. Nobody stopped him, so when he swung onto the Cross County Parkway he switched on his lights and made good time for home.

The Vardon house was dark when he braked to a halt. Ben and his wife Kathy would be asleep. His wrist watch showed twenty minutes past midnight. On shaking legs he walked up the flagstones to the front porch and pressed the bell.

On the third ring a window went up and a sleepy voice called, "Who's there?"

"Ben, it's me—Dan Kinnick. Somebody just tried to kill me!"

There was a little silence. Kinnick could hear Kathy saying, "At this hour?"

Then Ben called, "Be right down, Dan."

Ben Vardon was a big man, rawboned and heavyset. He had a wide face and high cheekbones. Kinnick thought there might be Indian blood in him from away back. He usually wore rumpled suits that were always unpressed and he carried anywhere from two to five pipes in his pockets. As he opened his front door, blinking sleepily in the glare from the street light, he looked neater in dark blue dressing gown and pajamas than he ever did dressed.

"You drunk, Dan?" His voice implied that he would not blame Kinnick if he were.

"There's a bullet hole in my car window," Kinnick said shakily. He was too nervous to be angry. "Come on, take a look at it." When the detective hesitated, he flared, "Goddam it! It's the only proof I got that something did happen to me!"

"Sure, Dan."

Vardon followed him along the walk to the car. He pursed his lips, looking at the hole, and muttered, "It's pretty big. Took a heavy bullet to make that hole. Maybe a .45 revolver or Colt automatic." He bent over and put his eye to the glass, sighting along it. "Just missed by a hair's whisker, didn't it? Shook you up some, I'll bet."

"I'm still shook," Kinnick agreed tightly.

"Sure. I can understand that. Come on in for coffee."

"No coffee. I just want to tell you what happened.

Maybe you know why somebody would want to kill me. I don't."

"Teen-agers?" Vardon asked with a quick glance.

Kinnick shook his head. "No, they were grown men. Big men, beefy, in neat hats and topcoats. I saw that much when that joe leaned out the window and fired."

"Recognize him if you saw him?"

"I don't think so. It was dark. It happened so fast—"

"Coffee," Ben said again, and this time he took Kinnick by the arm.

Kathy was waiting in the kitchen beside the stove, smiling cheerfully as if to hide the sympathy written on her face. She was small and pretty, with brown hair decorated with upwards of fifty bobby pins. When she saw his glance, she flushed and touched her hair, then shrugged.

"You've seen Midge like this a hundred times," she said.

Ben growled at her, and Kinnick knew they were trying to hide the sympathy they felt for him because of Midge. Right now he didn't want sympathy. He wanted explanations.

Vardon showed him into the breakfast nook bench and glowered down at him. "What can I tell you, Dan? Personally I think it was a case of mistaken identity. You drive a damn nice car, that new Holiday. A rich man's car. Somebody thought you were playing around with a wife, maybe."

Kinnick said flatly, "You know better'n that, Ben. There were two men in that car. Two men don't go around revenging one guy's horns."

"I was hoping you wouldn't notice that," Vardon grumbled. He sat across the table and leaned elbows on the formica tabletop. "I honestly don't know what the hell to tell you. I feel I know enough about you and your way of living to say nobody's got an excuse in God's wide world to blow your head off."

"Ben!" cried Kathy. His face was stony. "It's true, isn't it? Somebody did try to blow his head off. Dan wants to know why. So do I."

Vardon looked at Kinnick. "Tell me about it, just the way it happened."

Kinnick frowned. Where did you begin telling a man how you almost died? At the very moment when the bullet went by your jaw, or before that, when you brought Mrs. Conover the new battery for her car? Maybe the beginning should be somewhere else, in some forgotten moment out of time.

"I had a service call to make in the Bayswater Knoll section. At a Hamilton Avenue address. A Mrs. Conover. She had a run-down battery and I'd promised to bring her a new one, even as late as it was. I particularly remember she asked for an Auto-Lite. She saw an ad on television—"

Vardon looked impatient as Kinnick spread his hands. "I installed it and drove away. About a half-mile from her place—along Colonial Road—this Cadillac comes tear-assing past. A guy with a gun in his hand leaned out the window. I saw him from the corner of my eye. I jammed the anchors and felt the bullet skin my chin."

There was a little silence in the kitchen. Kinnick could hear the percolator bubbling. He said lamely, "That's about all, I guess."

Ben Vardon smiled wryly. "It's only the end, Dan. Now give me the beginning. Go back to where it all began. Go on. You can do it. Something inside you will tell you when to begin. . . ."

His voice trailed off and Kinnick sat hunched over, unaware that Kathy was at his elbow with the coffee pot. A beginning is a start of something, the very first link in the chain. Search back along these links of memory, Daniel Philip Kinnick, to the glistening first link, which was—

The robbery attempt that was no robbery at all?

Or the automobile plunging over the Ardsley Hill Road curve?

Midge? Did it commence with his wife?

No, it began after Midge, but before the accident. Maybe it was the last time he'd gone hunting up at Indian Head Lodge, the time he'd seen Donna Morrison. Kinnick scowled, remembering that afternoon and the man with the high-powered hunting rifle, the man with buck fever. . . .

The man was terrified. He whirled and threw the heavy Winchester from him as Kinnick came walking up the little slope, high grass swishing against his leather flight boots. There was a momentary flash of sunlight on glass and then the long ironweeds and gayfeathers hid the big hunting rifle.

The solitary hunter had eyes like black holes in his head and his forehead under the scarlet hunting cap was wet with sweat. Kinnick saw the shaking hands and smiled a little.

"Buck fever?" he asked gently.

The man took a deep, shuddering breath and nodded. "I guess so. I never had anything like it happen to me before. I—I saw the deer real good, right on my sights. It turned and—and looked at me and—"

Kinnick fumbled for cigarettes, bringing out the flat, silver case with his initials on it. He was a young man with very lean hips and wide, brawny shoulders under a blazing red jacket. There was a trace of blondish beard stubble at his jaw, and his lips were wide and curiously sensitive. He carried his Remington Magnum easily across his right forearm and offered the cigarette case with his left hand. The man took one with a grateful look.

"First time out?" asked Kinnick.

The man smiled tightly. "No, and I'm ashamed of myself. But I've never shot a deer, never even had one in my sights like that. I froze and started shaking. I think maybe I shook so much it made my gun go off. I don't remember squeezing the trigger."

"Buck fever can get anybody, beginner or old-timer. Never had it myself, but I was raised around these parts. My pop was a forest ranger. Hell, I grew up with deer running past our front door every morning."

Kinnick let smoke out of his nostrils and glanced idly across the dip of meadowland that lay between this ridge and the far slope of Mount Arrowhead, where fir and balsam grew so thickly that from this distance it looked like a shaggy green blanket. The early October day was crisp and clear with a hint of coming winter in the chill wind that roamed the highlands. His eye touched the gleaming brown stock of the fallen rifle. Only the stock showed. The rest of the gun was hidden by the tall grass.

"Better clean it off," he smiled, nodding at the Winchester. He shifted his own Magnum in the crook of his arm and said, "Guess I'll be running. Got to stop at the Lodge and settle up with Pops Morrison. Stayed overnight and had myself a few highballs."

The man nodded absentmindedly, staring out across the distant meadows. "Owe him some money myself. I'll be along shortly. Think I'll sit a while and get my breath."

Kinnick moved on up the hill, past a sprawling clump of white chickweed. He walked with steady strides, head down to watch his footing. Thinking about the man and his buck fever, he chuckled with sympathetic understanding. He might never have noticed him if the man hadn't fired. The sound of the shot roused him from his reveries, turning him from the beaten footpath and up into the tall shinleaf. He took a proprietary interest in what went on at the Morrison Lodge, probably because he'd been coming here since he was twelve and Donna Morrison only nine.

He was a married man now and should forget Donna, but how did one go about forgetting long black hair and the touch of soft lips in the night, the perfumed warmth of a first love? Or the long summer days and swimming in Vardis Lake, with hot dogs and cold soda pop waiting the stir of appetite? His mind could pick sounds and fragmentary sights out of the potpourri of memory— the touch of her hand in his as they tramped the autumn woods, the remembrance of laughter warmed by love, the togetherness of seeing the first spring robin or a ten-point buck—and revel in them.

Kinnick admitted honestly that he had been looking forward to meeting Donna this weekend; not out of any desire to be unfaithful to Midge, but from the bite of those inner hungers that assail a man when he feels he's growing older and that the carefree days of youth are only a bittersweetness in the mind.

"I'll be thirty next birthday," he muttered under his breath and wondered why he and Midge had never had children. Children might have made a difference in the way he and his wife got along.

He was moving past a hazel thicket and heading toward a fallen tree trunk when he realized that he had not felt this alive in months. The weight of the rifle on his arm, the biting October wind laden with the smell of wood-smoke, the sight of big yellow pumpkins in a distant field made a congestion of sense impressions that overwhelmed him. He came to a stop and breathed deep.

A man is a dull clod most of the time, but there are rare moments when his soul grows tumescently pleased with the world around him. Kinnick savored this instant of delight, wanting to hold on to it. A rail fence crisscrossed a strip of pasture three miles away; he could pick out the red leaves and berries of a cotoneaster clump as if they were within reaching distance. A bird doated lazily on a wind current beyond the rim of green-needled conifers. He could make out the red slate of the Lodge rooftiles, the other side of the next hill.

The sharpness of his senses fled unexpectedly and Kinnick experienced a sudden uneasiness. Turning, he searched his backtrail until he saw the man with buck fever, bulking big and solid in his hunting jacket, staring down at him. Kinnick lifted an arm and waved. The man turned and disappeared behind a patch of dogwood.

Kinnick shrugged and went on.

"Dan! Dan Kinnick!"

Donna Morrison was standing on the Lodge porch, sweatered arm lifted to him as he came across the macadam parking lot. She ran down the steps, laughing brightly, her long black hair gathered in a pony tail and bouncing wildly. His aliveness of a few minutes before came back with a rush.

She was as lovely as ever. Maybe more so, for her girlish body had filled out into rounded hips that pressed against carefully tailored black slacks, and he found himself pleasantly surprised at the fullness of her breasts. The years rolled away behind him. Dan Kinnick held out his arms, the Remington Magnum an unnoticed weight in his right hand.

"Donna! Ah, it's good to see you!"

He caught and hugged her, looking down into her sparkling eyes, and he knew, just before he bent his head, that he had to kiss her just as he had to breathe. Her lips were softly cradling, and the press of her middle against him was strangely disturbing. After a moment they realized they were in full view right smack in the middle of the Lodge parking lot, and drew away from each other.

"I was wild when Pops told me you'd come up yesterday and I wasn't here," she said, searching his face with hungry eyes. "I think I've been on and off that porch all day, waiting for you to come back. Oh, Dan, it's so good to talk to you again! Why've you stayed away so long?"

"Midge doesn't fancy my hunting trips."

"Oh." Her face was inscrutable. After a moment she asked, "How is Midge? How do you like married life? It's three years next April, isn't it?"

"Three years, yes."

"Happy years, Dan? No, I shouldn't ask that. It isn't any of my business. Come inside and have a whisky sour with me. You used to like the way I made them."

"Still do. Nobody can make one your way. It's something special." He hesitated then plunged on, "Just the way you're special, Donna."

She walked beside him with a free stride, smiling a little, turning her head to glance at him sideways out of the corners of her slanted eyes as she used to do. "Not special enough, though. I think that was the trouble with us, Dan. We were much too good friends to be in love. I was a pal, a gal to take to a dance or on a hay ride. I wasn't exciting—"

"Shut up, Donna," he growled and knew instant contrition. "I'm sorry. That slipped out."

"I'm glad it did," she said frankly. "It shows you've thought about me the way I've thought about you— wondering what went wrong between us."

"Nothing went wrong. I was a stupid fool."

Three years ago he had been mustered out of service, and was lonely. Midge had been a hostess at a fashionable restaurant in Mamaroneck just off U.S. 1. Twice a week and every weekend he ate there, always alone. They struck up a conversation and one night made a date to go dancing when she was through with work. He was lonely and she was tired of going home to an empty room, so after their drinks they went to a motel and registered as man and wife.

Looking back, Kinnick realized he was not the man to take a girl to a motel room and share a few hours of lovemaking without an insistent feeling of obligation. He was making good money as a mechanic in a Scarsdale garage—in service, he'd been an Air Force tech sergeant —so the morning after their fifth visit to the motel he proposed to her.

Somewhat to his surprise, she accepted him.

"Ever since, she's been trying to make me over to fit some kind of mental blueprint she has of what a husband ought to be," he said glumly, watching Donna pouring whisky into a cocktail shaker behind the Lodge bar. "I'd saved up my severance pay. She made me take it out and buy myself a service station in Yonkers. Told me I'd never get anywhere working for somebody else. Nothing satisfied her but that I own my own business. Since cars and machinery are the only thing I know—outside of guns and hunting—I did what she wanted."

Kinnick watched the gentle tremor of Donna's breasts as she shook the frosted glass shaker up and down. "Funny part of it is, I've done pretty well. I've more than doubled my old salary. I bought a new car. We threw our old furniture out and bought new for our apartment— we live in a two-family house on Pond Hill Road—and Midge buys as many new dresses as she wants. And she wants plenty."

He scowled into the whisky sour glass as Donna filled it. "This is my first vacation away from work since I bought the station. Maybe I wouldn't have taken even this weekend except that an old codger who used to work at the station hit me for a job the other day. He wants to do part-time work. So I took him on. Midge wasn't so keen on the idea, but—Lord, how I go on! Aren't you tired of listening?"

Donna leaned her elbows on the bartop, smiling with a peculiar twist of her full red mouth. "Use me, Dan. For a whipping boy. Get it out of your system." There was a warm tenderness in her eyes. "You men. Every one of you is a martyr. In you I like it."

"Hey, now," he protested. "I'm not exactly griping.

Don't get me wrong. Midge is a good kid. She has her faults—but hell—who doesn't? And how can you write off something that's worked out as well as the station has? Midge is making me a success in spite of myself."

He tasted the drink. It was smooth and as tartly sweet as any whisky sour she'd ever made. He told her so, then asked, "What about you? Last I remember, you were studying art."

"Four years at Skidmore. Now I'm a professional artist and teach at Midland High."

He straightened with a grin. "Honest Injun? Donna, that's great. An artist. How about that?"

"Care to see my etchings?"

"I do, soon's we do away with this shaker."

Her studio was the old Lodge stable, converted into an atelier by the ripping down of a shingled roof and the insertion of a slanted picture window. The wide-planked floor was painted gray and the thick upright beams were stained and waxed. A row of Afro-American wood carvings made grotesque curves and angles on a window ledge. Here and there Donna had hung wooden masks and plaques, carved from balsa or elm and painted with a delicate sensitivity to color.

"I'd never have believed Pops if he'd described this place to me," Kinnick enthused. "From the parking lot it looks like an abandoned stable."

"I have my own kitchen, my sitting room and a place to sleep. What more—outside a husband—could a girl ask?"

She brought him to a narrow staircase and up that to the open loft that long ago had stored hay and sacks of grain. An iron grille fence ran around the stable overhang. An easel and a modeling dais stood below the slanted window, directly in the bright yellow sunlight. An old paint-stained table and a highbacked chair with a fringed shawl flung across an arm added color to the setting. A row of unframed canvases leaned against the wall.

Donna lifted two of the oils and held them up for inspection as he lighted a cigarette. "A landscape and a still life. Someday you'll have to pose for me."

"You can call it 'Man Letting Down his Hair to Old

Girl Friend'," he nodded, blowing smoke. "I'll be glad to pose. Any time."

She came close and looked up at him. "Dan, was it my fault? I have to know. It means a lot to me."

Kinnick gestured aimlessly, in embarrassment. "It happened, Donna. If it was anybody's fault, it was mine. I forgot how wonderful you are."

Her mouth curved into a wistful smile. "I'd prefer to think you never knew how wonderful I could be, for you." She took the cigarette out of his mouth, the silver case from his fingers, putting them on the table. Then she moved forward until she was touching him at thighs and belly. Devil fires smoldered in her eyes as she lifted her arms and locked them about his neck. Now he felt the firm solidity of her breasts on his chest. "Call me what you want, Dan—but I have to know about us in the only way a poor, helpless female can tell."

Poor, helpless female? This woman he held in his arms was perfumed dynamite, ready to blow in half a hundred directions. Never before had he felt this crazy wildfire in his veins, not with Donna herself, and certainly never with Midge. He was a little giddy, he knew, as he bent to kiss her parting lips.

Her mouth was wide and hungry. Her moving tongue was a tender whip telling him he was a dumb damn fool to have let this girl get away from him. His hands went down her soft back and to her curving hips. Clinging, he pressed her even closer.

After a while, Kinnick grew aware that her fingernails were embedded in his shoulder, sharply biting through the tight weave of his red hunting shirt.

"You bastard," she whispered tenderly, making the word a caress. She kissed him lightly, just a brushing of her lips. "You should have married me. And it's too bad I'm a lady, or I'd take you away from your wife."

"Donna," he said, and then he stopped. What in hell could he say to this girl? Tell her that he knew she was right? That he'd been lonely when he got out of service and that he'd always considered her as a youngster, somebody outside his age group and not fair game for loving? He felt helpless.

Her eyes slanted at him, smoky and rebellious. "Or

maybe I'm just not enough of a bitch to make the play. Every woman is a bitch, darling. Didn't you know? Only some of us make believe we don't know it."

"Maybe I'd better be running."

She laughed softly. "Maybe you'd better, Dan. I'm a big girl now, though. Always remember it."

"You think I could forget?"

He let that hang between them as he went down the narrow stairs. He hefted his hunting jacket from a beam-peg and shrugged into it. His blood was pounding so heavily it made his ears pulse. When he went into the sunlight he was surprised to find it so bright. It seemed he'd been in the stable-studio a long time. Actually, it could have been only a few minutes.

Kinnick went into the Lodge and settled his bill. He turned over his rifle to Johnny Anson who clerked for Pops. Johnny was a crusty old bachelor who cleaned and polished the guns left in his care from one weekend to the next with the loving tenderness of a young mother with her firstborn. The next time he came through the Lodge door, Kinnick knew the Magnum would look as if it had just come out of a display window.

Standing in the doorway, he buttoned his jacket slowly, trying not to think about Donna Morrison. Moving across the porch he saw the man with buck fever come from be-tween two parked cars and walk toward him, carrying a Winchester M 71.

The man waved a hand and veered toward Kinnick. His face was flushed. Kinnick wondered if he'd been carrying a hip flask and had stopped along the trail to fortify his nerves. There was an almost jaunty air about him.

"Wanted to introduce myself and apologize for being so stupid back there on the ridge. Name's Fred Jackson. I'm in the trucking business up around White Plains." His hand clasp was firm and vigorous, but his smile seemed a little too fixed.

Kinnick said, "I run a gas station myself. In Yonkers. Not a big place—six pumps, a two-car repair garage. It's a living."

They had been walking beside the cars. When Kinnick turned in at his blue-gray Buick convertible, Jackson chuckled heavily. "Can't be too bad a living if you can afford a car like that."

"I can't afford it. My wife wanted it."

The red-faced man looked a little uncomfortable. He said, "Well, I just wanted to thank you for being so understanding. A lot of men would have laughed at me."

"Not a man who's ever hunted."

Kinnick could not explain it, but there was a need in him to get away from this smiling man. The more Jackson talked, the more uneasy Kinnick felt, as if he were hiding something with his speech.

As his foot pressed the starter, he grumbled, "I'm getting to be an old woman, for crissakes!" He wheeled the Century out of the strip and nursed it across the macadam to the big log gate.

He glanced in the rearview mirror. The red-faced man was still standing there, looking after him. Even while Kinnick stared, Jackson drew out a leatherbound notebook and pencil from an inner pocket and began to write on it.

CHAPTER TWO

Midge was still up when he got home an hour before midnight. She was wearing an imported French nightgown that was black lace from shoulders to navel and sheer black gauze below that. The heat had been turned up high and there was a smell of bubble bath and perfume in the air.

"Darling," she cried, waving a very white arm. "I feel *très gai*. Come share my wine cup."

The wine cup was a magnum of Pol Roger champagne, 1947 vintage, newly opened. It was only half-full. Midge sat curled in a heavily upholstered wing chair. Tiny pink feet peeped out from under the nightie hem. A pair of black mules with fluffy pompons lay on the rug before her.

"Well," said Kinnick. "Well, well."

"Very well, Danny boy."

She stood up and paraded around the room, letting her hips swing. "Like it, Danny? Like your Midge?"

"Like crazy, girl."

She considered that, blonde head tilted sideways, "I think you need a drink. You're too sober." There was a second flat-bottomed glass beside the champagne bottle on the end table. She bent and filled it, then brought it to him with both hands clasped under the bowl.

While he drank, she reached up and took off his hunting cap, then undid the buttons of his jacket.

In a small voice she asked, "Did you have a good time?"

"Great time. It was good to tramp through the woods. I haven't done it in ages, seems like."

"I'm glad." Her fingers were sly mice working his shirt

21

free, tugging it out of belted trousers. "I want you to feel free to go tramping through the woods if you want. Marriage isn't a jail, Danny. You mustn't ever feel like a prisoner."

His hands closed on her fingers, holding them on his belt-buckle. He was honestly puzzled, remembering the fight she'd put up before letting him drive off Saturday forenoon.

"What's the pitch, Midge?"

"Pitch?"

"The spiel, the play, the buildup. What's got into you? Since when is it okay for me to feel free to go off on a hunting trip?"

She pouted, looking hurt. "I've been all alone since Saturday noon. I had time to think about us. I've been a pretty terrible wife, haven't I, Dan? Always harping about getting somewhere in life, making you keep your nose to the grindstone." She looked down at her glass, then raised it to her lips. When the champagne was gone she smiled at him.

"I drank a whole magnum after I took my bath. I wanted to get tiddley. I don't want anything to happen to our marriage, Dan."

He said, "Nothing's going to happen. If you'd only stop buying so damn much—give me a chance to build up a bank account—maybe I could see the point to working so hard."

She put down the champagne glass and came against him, lifting her arms to put them around him. Kinnick felt the hard tips of her breasts against his chest.

"We're young, honey. Let's live a little before we start thinking about bank accounts. You want to be proud of me, don't you? You want me to wear nice clothes. Folks don't judge a man's success by what he wears, but by what his wife wears. Or what she doesn't wear."

Her nearness, the touch of smooth flesh under the thin black gauze wore down his suspicions. "I wish you meant all this, just the way it sounds. I honest to God do," he said, letting his palms stroke her hips.

She was leaning into him, suspending her weight from the hands clasped behind his neck. Blue eye shadow made purple enigmas of her eyes, and she'd run lipstick over her mouth with a heavy hand. Even her perfume was headier than usual. She was more the girl he'd married than she'd been in a long time.

When he told her this, she made a throaty sound and closed her eyes, moving tighter in to him. "I want to be your bride, Danny. That's the way I want you to think about me, all the time. Even when you're off on a—on a hunting trip."

He caught the faint inflection of her voice and wondered, but she was so near and her lips so ripe that he forgot everything before a compulsive urge to kiss her. When she bit his tongue very gently, he began to tremble.

"Take a shower, honey. I'm going to make martinis."

"Yeah," he said gustily. "Right away."

When the steam was rising like white mist around him in the shower stall he heard the bathroom door open. "Turn off the water, darling," she called, and an instant later the frosted glass shower door opened to permit her hand to move in with a cocktail glass.

When he swallowed it, and handed it back, there was another. "Hey, what gives? You'll get me starry eyed."

Her giggle made music. "Just the way I want you, bridegroom. Now take your medicine. Mamma'll be waiting."

Kinnick began to sing, off key and loudly. He could not remember the last time he'd bellowed like this in a shower. Maybe it was a good sign. Maybe he and Midge were starting a new road together and were going to hit it off better than they ever had before. The idea made him feel good.

He walked into their bedroom with the towel draped about him. Midge lay with her back propped to the headboard, smiling lazily. The black nightgown was pulled up to her hips, revealing shapely legs.

"Hello, bridegroom," she whispered.

"Hello, bride," he smiled, and dropped the towel.

The single lamp on the night table still burned as Midge rose on an elbow to look down into his face. Kinnick was empty of everything but slumbrous lassitude. The clock radio told him it was twenty minutes after three in the morning. He lay back wearily and closed his eyes.

"Lover," she whispered and kissed the corner of his mouth.

"Dead lover," he grunted. "Woman, you are insatiable."

"Thank you, dear." After a moment, "Danny?"

"Mmmmmm?"

"What girl did you meet up at the Lodge?"

He opened one eye and stared at her. "Girl? What girl?"

A red-nailed finger made little circles on his chest. Behind the long yellow lashes her eyes were downcast. "The girl who lives at the Lodge. I don't know her name."

He was silent a moment. Then he said, "What I can't figure out is how you know about her at all. But don't tell me. Let me guess. You trailed me disguised as a dogwood tree."

"Danny, I'm serious!"

"Or you hired a private eye who gave you his report just as I pulled out of the Lodge parking lot. Maybe your mother was a witch and owned a magic Ouija board that you inherited. Am I getting warm?"

"A man named Jackson called me up."

His eyes opened and he stared at her. "Fred Jackson? The man with buck fever?" He told her about seeing Jackson.

"He said he'd met you. He didn't tell me how. There was something in his voice I didn't like, Danny. Especially when he told me how you kissed that pretty girl in the parking lot right where everybody could see you."

"Goddam peeping tom!"

"Who is she, darling?"

"An old girl friend. I haven't seen her in four, five years. Sure I kissed her. Hell, I kissed your mother when I met her, too."

There was a silence. In a small voice, Midge said, "You went into her studio, too."

Kinnick laughed. "If I didn't know Jackson was in the trucking line I'd say he was a detective. What else did he tell you?"

"That you forgot your cigarette case, the one I gave you, the one with our initials on it. You left it in her studio. You must have been pretty excited to do that, Danny."

He stared up into her troubled face and felt tenderness wash over him. His hand sought hers, brought the soft palm to his lips. "Honey, I've never even thought about another girl since we got married. God's gospel."

"Until this weekend. The man said she came running out with your cigarette case, but you'd gone. She must have been excited herself or upset, not to notice it. I would have noticed it, Danny. This Fred Jackson said he lives down our way and that if she gave the case to him, he'd see you got it. The girl was reluctant to give it to him. Why, Danny?"

"Maybe she didn't trust the bastard."

"Why are you so angry with him? Is there something you did I shouldn't know about? Is that it?"

"Look, I only kissed the girl. I didn't stay and raise a family. Now let's get to sleep. It's my turn to open up the station tomorrow."

Her fingers caught the thick hairs on his chest and tugged. "I'm not really angry, just hurt. But I want to talk about it. I want you to reassure me that's all it was between you and this girl. Just an old friendship."

"It was just an old friendship."

"You don't sound very convincing."

Kinnick sighed. "If your new friend was such a good detective, why didn't he tell you I was in her studio only about three minutes? What the hell could happen in that time?"

Midge smiled faintly. "He took very great pains to tell me you weren't in there very long. He was being very much the man of the world, laughing and joking about it, assuring me nothing had happened in all probability—he said that, 'in all probability'—and not to worry. He learned your name and address and phone number from somebody called Pops, and decided to let you know he had the cigarette case and would mail it first thing Monday morning."

"Being a real big help, wasn't he? Why, for God's sake?"

Midge pouted. "I think he was very nice. I told him so. He even said I was a wonderful wife to be so understanding."

"And you are." He leaned over and kissed her. "Now

be even more wonderful and let me go to sleep." Tiredness was an ache in the back of his neck, in the tight muscles of legs and belly.

Midge sighed and got out of bed for her nightgown.

And since that night with Midge, what is there to remember, Daniel Philip Kinnick? Search deep into your mind and memory for the words and actions that may give an answer to the riddle of this night when you almost died. Go deep, go deep: swimming through chaos and the fragments of lost days and forgotten nights, hunting substantiality in a web of gossamer. You need building blocks in this world of colored lights and empty bubbles, but there are no rocks, no stones, no lengths of solid wood. Only illusion and the touch of nightmare. . . .

The days ran on into weeks, and early fall became late autumn. Dry brown leaves rustled underfoot. Woodsmoke was a haze in the air. Topcoats came out of moth chests and closets, and women began showing their fur coats. More and more cars were stopping off at the station for winterizing and oil changes. Dan Kinnick had little time to think of anything but work, these days. Willie Magruder was coming in four, five days, a week now to run the gas pumps and do little jobs like changing flats or adjusting a carburetor now and then.

Midge was always waiting for him at night with a hot meal and a kiss. He was glad to see her looking so well. It seemed she was taking more care of her personal appearance than she'd ever done before. Usually she lazed around the house in a kimono or linen wrapper, but now she was immaculate in tight sheaths or a white jersey cocktail dress with a wide band of white satin that gave her middle an almost tiny look. There were floor-length culottes and a sleeveless cowl-necked jacket that she wore on some occasions, too.

"I'm your bride, Danny," she informed him when he complimented her. "I can't have old girl friends crushing you in their arms every time they see you, now can I?"

By this time, his hunting trip was a joke between them. The cigarette case had arrived in the morning mail as promised, Midge told him. It had come with a note from

Fred Jackson, written on an office letterhead with the inscription *JACKSON AND TRUBO, modern truckers* as its masthead. He wrote a big, scrawly hand, and Kinnick thought it the handwriting of a man in a hurry and going places.

It snowed the day after Thanksgiving. Kinnick was at the station until all hours for the next few days, putting on snow tires, selling chains, pouring Prestone and alcohol into radiators. Sometimes it was close to midnight when he got home.

One night he met Thyra Prentice in the lower hall, putting out milk bottles. The Prentices owned the two-story, two-family house where he lived. Thyra was their only child, a girl in her late twenties, with thick black hair, and pretty in a fleshy sort of way. Kinnick knew she was popular with the boys. Nights he came home early he could hear her running back and forth below, calling out that she'd be ready in a minute, and then her high heels would be in the hallway with her date, and the door would close behind them. After they'd gone, the house always seemed a little lonelier to him.

"Oh, you scared me," she said from her hunkered down position beside the milkbox. Then she smiled in a friendly way, not noticing that her bathrobe was gaping just enough to show a white knee and part of a smooth thigh. He wondered if she was wearing anything under the woolen robe.

She straightened slowly and drew the wrapper around her until it was tight over the twin mounds of her bosom. She had full breasts, and Kinnick could understand why she was so popular with the young males of Westchester County. What he couldn't understand was why she'd never married.

"You must be beat," she said. "Working day and night in that gas station. There're rings under your eyes."

"All I need's a good night's sleep."

"Why work so hard? Life is to have fun."

"I got responsibilities. A wife and a business."

A funny look crossed her face, as if a shadow startled her. "Your wife. Oh, yes. She has fun. Why don't you?"

"Midge?" he asked in surprise. "She's worse off than I am, cooped up all the time in the apartment."

"She went out tonight around seven."

"I know about that," he lied. "The place she used to work is giving a party for a girl getting married. She was invited."

His words were coming out of left field, off the top of his head. If Midge were not upstairs, he didn't know where she was. He felt vaguely worried.

Thyra Prentice smiled amusedly. "Whatever you say, Mr. Kinnick." Her hand sought the knob of her apartment door and she slid inside. Before closing it, she smiled at him again. "Night now. Pleasant dreams."

Kinnick shook his head, smiling a little, and went upstairs. The apartment was dark and empty. He turned on the wall lights in the living room then went into the kitchen, switching on the overhead electrics. For some reason, he wanted plenty of light. There were three cans of Schlitz in the refrigerator, cold enough to sting the fingers. He found a wedge of Provolone and some crackers, and sat eating with one eye on the red kitchen wall-clock.

It was ten after one when a key slid into the front door lock. A moment later Midge rushed into the kitchen, her face an apologetic mask.

"Honey, I'm so sorry! Mabel Hunter asked me to go out with her. Her mother's sick and Mabe hasn't stirred out for ages. We went to a drive-in up in Elmsford and got a flat tire. I thought I'd be back long before this."

"You get pretty dolled up for a date with Mabel Hunter," he commented, eying the black shirtwaist dress and heavy silver ring and bracelet as she shrugged out of the Russian broadtail coat.

Midge laughed gaily. "Darling if you could have heard me praising you—telling Mabe and her mother what a go-getter you are—how you absolutely insist on my wearing the very latest fashions—" She broke off and looked hurt. "You do want me to look my best, don't you?"

"Sure, sure. Only it seems a little overdone, dressing up like that just to go to a movie."

Her hand patted his cheek as she pressed against him. "You just don't understand us girls, darling. We're bitches, all of us. If we get something new, we're not satisfied until we've shown it around among our female friends, meowing very politely, as if to say, 'Ah-hah, look what I have that you don't.' Don't give it any more thought."

She turned her back. "Unzip me, Danny. Tired?"

"Beat to the ears."

"Too bad. I have on a new bra and panty set. I thought you might like to admire it. But if—"

The zipper was undone to below her middle. Kinnick could see a blue brassiere strap banding her back and the lacy top of transparent briefs. He grinned and walloped her backside.

"I'm never that tired."

Nor was he.

Think hard, Daniel Philip Kinnick!

What else can you remember about the days of working at the gas station and the nights of coming home exhausted to Midge? Life can become an unmeaning endlessness of light and dark and busy hands after a while, in which auto wheels go flying through a bubbly place like flying saucers, and carburetors swollen to monstrous size war with cylinder heads and bodiless fanwheels. Too much work can dim the mind, making it a vacant nothingness filled only with sense impressions and animal urges.

Deep in those sense impressions or lost in the animal urges that belong to every man is the clue you need. . . .

Perhaps it was the robbery that was no robbery.

CHAPTER THREE

The money was in the cash register.

It was a wrong note, and Kinnick did not like wrong notes. The money should be gone and the cash drawer empty. Otherwise there was no way to explain the scratch marks on the metal sill of the casement window.

He went to the window and examined the marks again. They were shallow and bright where the paint had scraped away. He'd never even seen pictures of jimmies, let alone the real thing, and he didn't know whether modern sneak-thieves used them, but he had the feeling that a jimmy might have made the marks.

"Whoever it was got in here all right. There's a footprint near the desk where he must have stepped. But he didn't take the money."

Kinnick reflected that he never locked his cash register, always leaving a small amount of loose change and some dollar bills in the drawers, preferring to take a small loss rather than have the expensive cash register broken. In a way, it was like insurance. But the thief had ignored the cash register.

He sat on the edge of his desk and reached for the phone, dialing the Wells Avenue number of the Yonkers police department. There was the distant whirr of telephone bell and then a hoarse voice said, "Detective Bureau."

"I'd like to speak to Ben Vardon. Detective-Sergeant Vardon." After a little pause in which Kinnick heard voices, Ben came to the phone. He told Ben what had happened, making it slow and careful, so as not to forget anything.

Ben was amused. "Somebody scared him off. Maybe a prowl car. The boys stop off at business places and move a flash around a window. He probably heard them and got cold feet."

"Maybe. I suppose you're right."

"Anything missing? Some cans of oil or snow tires? Stuff like that?"

Kinnick had not checked, and felt embarrassed. Ben laughed. "Tell you what, Dan. Give me fifteen minutes. We'll go over the place together."

"Swell, Ben. And thanks."

A customer pulled in at the high-test pump, and Kinnick went out and unhooked the feeder. He remarked about the weather and Jim Henderson's boy Ed who was going great guns playing football for Roosevelt High. He went through the motions automatically: cleanser on the windshield, wipe with tissue, check water, oil and battery. It was routine, and he did it mechanically, without thinking.

Two more men pulled in, and he was so busy with them that he was surprised when Ben Vardon leaned out a window of his '56 Ford and said, "I'm reporting on the great gas station break-in, sir. May I have your name, sir?"

Kinnick laughed and went over to the car, leaning an elbow on the window ledge. "So I'm a psychopathic worrier. Get out of there and start earning your salary."

"I started earning it before I left the office. I called the desk sergeant at the second precinct. One of his prowl car men checked the station around midnight, and reported nothing suspicious at that time."

"Then it was broken into after midnight?"

Ben shook his head. "Maybe. We can't be sure." He came out of the car and walked toward the white picket fence that bordered the east side of the station.

Between the fence and the white stucco station wall was a narrow space filled with snow and ice. There was one window in the otherwise unbroken expanse of wall. Ben said, "This leads into your office, right? The garage is back the other side."

"The station runs north and south, with the garage on the south side," Kinnick said. "The place is mostly garage. The office is for incidental supplies. You know, oil, spark plugs, fan belts. That sort of thing."

Ben grunted. He walked beside the picket fence, tramping in the snow, then turned to follow it along the property line. He came out on the apron in front of the garage's double doors. Kinnick walked after him.

"Garage doors locked?"

"I tested them soon's I found the window open. They're still locked."

"Nothing missing inside?"

"Nothing I could see. I haven't checked everything."

"Well, come on. Let's go check."

The front office was neat and clean. The cement floor was painted a dark green, the walls an off-white. Shelves ranged the walls behind the office desk and chair, and along the west wall. A big window with gold lettering that read KINNICK SERVICE STATION gave a full view of the tank apron. Vardon stared into the display shelf where three pyramids of golden oil cans stood outlined against a green crepe-paper background. He turned to run his gaze along the wall shelves.

"Everything seems in order," he said slowly.

He went and looked at the muddy footprint beside the desk. "Snowed last night. That would explain the wetness and the mud. I'll send a man out to take a few pictures. Don't touch anything. What's in the garage?"

"Just my car." Kinnick moved through the metal door to the garage. His hand gestured at the late-model Buick Century.

Workbenches lined three walls of the garage. A work-pit was fitted with a hydraulic lift. A few tools lay on its floor where Kinnick had left them yesterday at closing. Overhead rack-beams held new tires. Beyond the three metal posts supporting the flat roof was the Buick.

The hose-bell sounded. "Got a customer," Kinnick said. "Be right back."

"Take your time. I'll mosey around."

When he finished with his customer, Kinnick saw Vardon coming through the office door. The detective scowled while he fumbled for a pipe and a sack of Golden Cavendish tobacco in his coat pockets.

"I couldn't find anything wrong, Dan. Looks to me

as if our friend got cold feet after he got in and beat it
without taking anything. I'll make out my report that
way, if it's all right with you."

"You know your job, Ben. I'm glad you came out.
Makes me feel better. I still think there's something inside we both missed, though."

Vardon had his pipe going. He grinned, "You find anything, let me know." His attitude was casual. Kinnick
decided he was thinking, I see a dozen break-ins during
a normal day and this is just one more for the blotter.
Nothing special about it, except the owner is luckier
than most. This crook didn't take anything. Vardon
waved a hand as he turned off the apron onto Yonkers
Avenue.

The telephone rang.

It was Midge.

"Danny, honey? You haven't forgotten you promised
me the car, have you?"

"Sure, Midge. But you know I got to make a repair
call just as soon as Willie gets here. It's—" he turned
and glanced at the desk clock, "only eight-thirty. Suppose I run up to Hartwell's on that fix-up job and get
back by eleven. You won't want—"

"But I will, Danny. I'm going to get dressed right
away. I'll be over before nine. Honey? You did promise."

Kinnick could picture her sprawled back in the bed-
covers, two pillows propped behind her, yellow hair
tousled around her pretty face. She was wearing the
blue short-nighty—thirty dollars in Lord and Taylor, but
seeing Midge in it was worth every penny of the price
—and if the covers were pushed down, her slim legs
would be showing from painted toenails to hips. He
thought about those legs a moment, then said, "Okay,
hon. I'll back it out for you."

Willie Magruder came in the front door. He was a
dour Scotchman somewhere between sixty and eighty
years of age. Kinnick could never tell exactly, because
the old man was ramrod straight and energetic, with a
strange little hop to his stride that was oddly youthful,
and his gaze was brightly alert. He was a magician with
a tool kit and knew an automobile from front bumper
to taillight, though he preferred the easier jobs. Healthy

as a lion, he was always complaining of what he termed
the miseries; but when Dan Kinnick found himself
stumped by a balky generator, Willie was not above
pitching in with his sleeves rolled high on still-brawny
arms.

"Ar," he grunted, which was a fair speech for Willie.

Kinnick placed the phone on its cradle and swung off
the desk. He told the Scotchman about the robbery attempt. Willie shook his head and made comments about
the lawlessness of youth.

"You think that's what it was? Kids?"

"Wha' else?"

The old man busied himself with a crate of oil cans,
ripping open the container and setting the glistening
golden cans in neat stacks on a shelf. Kinnick watched
him a moment, thinking, that could be it. Kids, out for
some fun. They'd scatter fast enough if a prowl car
pulled in and a cop sent a flashlight beam into the office.
Kids. Sure! No self-respecting burglar would bother about
the peanuts to be picked up in a closed gas station. It
would explain why the money was still in the drawer,
too. A youngster would panic easier than an old hand.

Feeling somewhat better, Kinnick went into the garage,
unlocked and lifted the overhead door and got into the
Century. A foot on the gas pedal, he let the motor
warm, then backed the convertible out onto the apron.

As he slid from the seat he saw Midge coming across
Oliver Street, walking in her bouncy stride. He stood
and watched her come to him, all perfume and new
clothes and the rich Russian broadtail. Pride of owner-
ship made him glow a little. His eyes looked at the trees
and off down the street, and inside him a voice was
saying, take a look at what cooks my meals and warms
my bed for me, world! This is my female, my mate!
It was a good feeling. Ever since that time he'd gone
hunting, she'd been different.

Kinnick smiled to himself. Does a woman good, sometimes, to learn other dames might like to kiss their old-
hat husbands. Sort of puts her on her mettle. They never
fought any more, the way they used to. Midge seemed
satisfied now with the money he brought in. Well, hell,
why shouldn't she, with him netting close to two hun-

dred a week? And she was more loving, always showing off her shape in frilly underthings or night garments, hungry for his compliments, his caresses.

Just like now, coming right up to him and putting her mouth to his, not caring whether her lipstick smeared or not, giving him a hint of expensive Schiaparelli *Shocking*. "Be back before three, honey. Just running up to do a little shopping and maybe have lunch with Mabel."

"Have fun. Watch out for ice patches."

It had snowed fairly heavily last night for the third time since Thanksgiving. The snowplows had gone through early in the morning, but there was snow and ice on the back streets. Along the curbs, piled snow made small mountains. Where traffic packed the snow down, freezing weather had turned it to ice. The roads were slippery and dangerous without chains or snow tires.

"I'm not going any back way, Danny. Up Central and over Ardsley Avenue Hill to Scarsdale to meet Mabe, then on to White Plains."

She was in the driver's seat, slippered foot pressing down on the starter, wriggling gloved fingers at him, pursing her mouth to blow a kiss. Kinnick watched her back into Oliver, then round the corner onto Yonkers Avenue. He caught a flash of her upraised hand as the Buick slid forward, gathering speed and momentum.   ·

Kinnick whistled as he closed the garage overhead.

It was a busy day just as they all were, lately. Kinnick was glad he was working so hard. Every penny earned meant a penny more for Midge. They had close to two thousand in the savings bank and almost five hundred in the checking account, despite the new convertible and all the clothes Midge bought. Their next step upward was a new home, maybe over in Secor Farms in Scarsdale or the Saxon Woods section of Mamaroneck. Maybe a kid or two, by that time, too. He wasn't getting any younger. If he were going to teach a youngster how to throw a nickel curve or boot a drop kick, he and Midge'd better start having them before he got so old and crotchety he wouldn't want to do anything but work and sleep.

The telephone rang while he was making change from

a brand-new double sawbuck. He reached for it idly, eyes intent on the man in the expensive tweed topcoat chewing a two-dollar cigar and waiting impatiently for his change.

"Kinnick Service Station. Dan Kinnick."

"Dan, it's Ben Vardon."

"Changed your mind about the robbery, did you?"

"No, it's something else." The voice was faint and far away, and there was a curious kind of lifelessness in it that made Kinnick straighten slowly.

He said, "Yeah? Well go ahead, boy."

"It's Midge, Dan. She's dead."

The big man with the two-dollar cigar turned and stared through the big plate-glass window into the office. Kinnick found his eyes caught and held by the smoke rising from the cigar, even as his insides began to turn. Twice he tried to talk, but his lips would not open.

"Dan? She went over Ardsley Avenue Hill, through a wooden fence and fell fifty feet. The convertible upended on her. The top—what the hell kind of protection is a canvas top?—wasn't any help. She died right away. There wasn't any—no pain, that is, Dan. It's something to be glad for."

"Yeah," he said. "Yeah, sure. Thanks, Ben."

He put the telephone back on its cradle and finished making change of the twenty. Opening the door, he stepped out and handed the man his money. There was a terrible impulse in him to cry, but he fought it back. Midge. His Midge, dead? No, no, it wasn't true. It couldn't be true. Somebody'd made a mistake. He didn't own the only Buick convertible in Westchester County.

Ben Vardon would not make a mistake, though. Not in something as important as this. "My God," he whispered, and felt his throat swell up.

He ran for the office, banging open the door, screaming at Willie Magruder in the repair shop, "Midge just got killed. Midge just got killed. The car went off the Ardsley Avenue Hill!"

"Go' above," whispered Willie, eyes round.

"I'm taking your jeep. I got to go there."

As he was backing the jeep onto the apron, a police motorcycle trundled to a stop beside the curb. A white-helmeted officer with a face wind-red behind colored goggles called out, "You Dan Kinnick? Ben Vardon sent me. You can follow me."

They went screaming up to Scarsdale at over eighty, the motorcycle siren brushing traffic aside as if it were a flailing hand. Kinnick rode with his foot on the floorboard, coaxing the last bit of energy out of Willie's jeep.

Vardon met him at the edge of the gully where sheer wall formed the support for this section of the Ardsley Avenue thoroughfare. Fifty feet above them a splintered wooden fence showed the force with which the car had hurtled through it. Kinnick felt his eyes drawn to the overturned car, the sheeted figure lying so motionless beside it.

Ben said softly, "I knew you'd want to come, Dan. But for God's sake don't go any closer."

"That bad?"

"It's that bad."

He swallowed hard, wondering where his heart had gone. After a moment he asked, "What happened? Does anybody know?"

"Man behind her named John Young witnessed the whole thing. He said the car skidded and went out of control. She was doing maybe forty, maybe forty-five. Too fast for that hill in this weather, though it was sanded down. She was coming downhill, so that might have made a difference. The car hit the fence and went through like it was tissue paper."

Kinnick closed his eyes, trying not to think how Midge must have felt all alone as the wood splintered and there was nothing beneath her but fifty feet of emptiness and the waiting gully rocks, with the convertible turning over slowly and throwing her into the canvas top just before it hit. It must have been fast. There would have been no time to think or even scream. Midge was a good driver. She would have been fighting the slide for all she was worth, not thinking about anything but getting control of the car back into her hands.

Vardon had a hand on his arm, squeezing it tight. "Let me handle things, Dan. You go on home. Or better, go back to work."

He wanted to ask, how the hell can I work? but he knew Vardon meant well, and anyhow, what do you say to a man at a time like this? He mumbled thickly, not making any sense even to himself, letting the detective turn him back toward the jeep.

"Work will keep you from thinking about it too much, Dan. You know that, don't you? I'll make all the arrangements. Funeral parlor and all, I mean. Just leave things to me."

"Sure, sure."

He sat in the jeep with his hands knotted about the steering wheel for what seemed like an eternity with Vardon standing motionless, looking at him with sad eyes. An imp inside him howled with satanic glee. You worked all the time when Midge was alive, now you got to work even harder because she's dead, to forget! He wished he could forget he was a man and cry the tears that were frozen away inside him.

What now, Daniel Philip Kinnick? Midge lies buried in her casket, but you live and walk about. You have your freedom now. What have you done with it? Did you use that freedom to make an enemy, someone who hates you enough to try and put a bullet in you? Did you have yourself a fling to drown the silver strands of loneliness or just for the sheer hell of being alive? No, no. You have led a quiet life since your wife died. Nobody hates you. There is no reason for anyone to want you dead like Midge.

You tell yourself all this, but a pallid blue mist of fear creeps into your empty days and nights. As a caged animal may in the first moments of its captivity, your soul screams in rage and terror. Being a man, you hide it in ordinary, workaday affairs. . . .

CHAPTER FOUR

Kinnick never knew how he got through the next few days. All his life he'd had a dread of funeral homes. Now he had to stand beside the ornate mahogany and silver casket that held the woman who had been his wife and accept the whispered condolences of a lot of people he'd never seen before. The flowers gave off a sickishly sweet perfume. The air was close inside the parlor. After a while he got a dull, throbbing headache.

His mornings he spent at the garage trying to work, to shake off the sense of disbelief that gripped him. Midge was not dead. She was too young to die, too pretty. It was all a ghastly mistake. He would wake up pretty soon and she would be beside him in bed, and he would take her in his arms and kiss her.

Only he didn't wake up.

A man named Purcell tried to reach him by telephone at the garage. Willie Magruder couldn't tell him what the man wanted.

The pretty widow who lived down the block from him, who had two small children and whose husband had been a fighter-pilot in Korea before going down in flames along Mig Alley, stopped by with a hot lunch and an invitation to come to dinner some night soon at her house.

Max Sigratty who owned the corner bar and grille came in with a fifth of Irish whisky. He told Kinnick to get as drunk as he had done when his own wife died three years back. He knew how Dan felt. He'd been all through it.

On the night before the funeral, Donna Morrison came into the parlor. There were tears in her dark eyes as

39

she clasped his hand. "I'm so sorry, Dan. There isn't anything anybody can say."

He forced a grin. "Thanks for driving down, Donna. Where are you staying?"

"At a motel off the Thruway," she told him.

"I'll see you home there."

"No, Dan. I wish you wouldn't. I wouldn't feel right about it. Not now."

"All right. If you say so."

Her smile was wistful. "But I would like to see you again, soon. I mean—don't be a stranger now that you don't have to stay away."

"I won't, I promise. And I'm glad you came. There are a lot of folks here—Midge's friends—I've never seen before. It's good to see an old friend."

"I'll stay over for the funeral. Afterward, I'm going back to the Lodge. Maybe in a couple of weeks I'll come down again. You can buy me a drink then, if you will."

"Sure. Sure thing, Donna."

He stood on the sidewalk and watched her slide across the seat of her blue Comet. He closed the door behind her gently. The closing of a door is often symbolical of an ending. The thought came unbidden to him that in this instance, it might herald a beginning.

The day of the funeral was raw and cold, with a threat of more snow in the gray sky. A lonely kind of day, Kinnick thought. Years ago, he'd liked nothing better than to tramp the woods by himself under leaden skies like these, listening to the gentle bubble of a mountain brook and to the rasp of dry tree branches brushed together by the wind. It was even more lonely, now.

As he watched the casket being lowered into the ground, there was no emotion in him. This was a time for grief, but he had no grief. It was just as if he were dead inside, like a lump of putty. Maybe this deadness was the only true sorrow, though. He didn't know and he didn't want to think about it.

There was a little stir beside the grave. The people were going now, drawing their coats tighter as if to shake away the oppressive heaviness of spirit. One by one they came up to Dan Kinnick and took his hand. Max Sagratty was there and the pretty widow, with Willie

Magruder and half a dozen friends of Midge's, including Mabel Hunter and her mother. Donna Morrison was subdued and withdrawn in a simple black chemise dress and Persian lamb coat, a tiny feathered black toque on her head.

She held his hand a moment, whispering, "Come up to the Lodge for a while, Dan. It'll be good for you." She smiled faintly, as if tired. "If you don't, I'll come down here. We won't stay away as long as we did after you went in the Army."

A lean man stood behind her, his cheeks fallen-in and cadaverous looking. "No time for me to see you, Kinnick. Name's Purcell. I'll be around at your garage in a day or two."

There were other neighbors, men and women he was surprised to see here at the grave, like the Meldrums who owned the little delicatessen on the corner, the Fitzgeralds who ran the Cadillac agency, the Tastrums, the Otises. Even the plump widow had made it her business to be here. Dan wondered with a wry smile at himself if she might be window-shopping for a husband. Fingers caught his arm, shaking him free of his wandering thoughts as more of these people who had shared a little part of his life with Midge came to add their sympathies to those of the others.

Ben Vardon was waiting just outside the iron grille gates in a squad car. His face was set in a hard frown.

"Dan, this is one hell of a time to bother you, but something's come up. Did you know Midge carried a big life insurance policy?"

Kinnick was honestly surprised. "Insurance policy? No, I didn't."

"For twenty thousand bucks. There was an accidental death clause in it. If the company's satisfied she met an accidental death, it pays double. Forty grand. A lot of moola, boy. It may make the insurance company suspicious."

For a moment Kinnick stared before he felt the slow tide of anger rise into his flushed cheeks. "Are you trying to tell me maybe I *murdered* Midge, Ben?"

"Not me, no. But this insurance character Purcell has been asking questions down at headquarters. He went to see John Young who witnessed the accident. He's gone over our blotter with a fine-tooth comb."

Kinnick fought down his fury, shaking his head slowly. "Hell, let him keep his goddam money. I don't want it."

"Look, Dan. I'm your friend. I know you and I knew Midge. We all used to go out together. You wouldn't and didn't kill her. But this Purcell doesn't know that. It's his business to go poking his nose into people's affairs. It's the way he earns his living. I stopped by to let you know, to warn you to keep your head with him. Don't fly off the handle."

"Purcell? Sure, that's the name. He's been phoning to the garage, trying to pump Willie, I guess." He grinned tightly, forcing his facial muscles. "He might as well try to pump a stone. Well, I guess I'll be the next guy on his stop list. I'll be expecting him, Ben. And thanks for dropping by."

He watched the squad car pull away with a scrape of tires on gravel. A realization that this was the end of the trail came over him. He would never see Midge again. She was behind him, in back of the grille fence, forever. For the first time he seemed to grow aware that she was dead. No more Midge. No more happy laughter, no more parading around to be admired, no more champagne magnums to be shared.

End. *Fine. Finis.*

He could not go back to the garage. Tomorrow would be time enough for that. Nor could he go home to the empty apartment. Not until tonight, late tonight. Instead, he would walk through the winter woods and breathe the clean fresh air, and look at the blue sky and the white clouds and know he was not the only person in the world ever to have lost someone dear to him. It would be like going to church.

Three days after the funeral, Purcell came to see him. He bulked tall and lanky in the garage doorway one morning, a briefcase in his right hand, a sad look in his eyes.

"Mr. Kinnick? Daniel Philip Kinnick?"

Dan looked up from the motor of a Cadillac where

he'd been installing new spark plugs. He moved his hands on the wipe rag, waiting.

"James Purcell is my name. I'm from Aetna." He held out a card. Dan took it, glancing at the printed words. The man looked around the garage. "It's about your wife, the late Mrs. Kinnick."

"Yeah," said Dan. "Yeah, sure. Come on inside."

He closed the office door behind him, telling Willie not to interrupt them. His hand motioned the insurance adjuster toward the desk chair. Kinnick wanted to stand, for some reason. He told himself not to get tense or tight. He had nothing to do with Midge's death. All he need do was answer a few questions.

"You know your wife carried a sizable policy with—"

"I didn't know that, no. Not until Ben Vardon told me about it. Midge must have paid the premiums on her own. I had nothing to do with them."

Purcell smiled and nodded. "As far as our records go, that is correct. Mrs. Kinnick always paid by cash. She took out the policy five years before you were married. Until the date of your marriage her beneficiary was her mother. She made you her beneficiary two weeks after you got married. She never told you?"

"Never."

Kinnick forced himself to relax. The tightness was in his throat like a hand squeezing, and the other man could sense it. Purcell pursed his lips and shook his head slowly.

"Most unusual. Most irregular. Wives always turn over their policies to their husbands when they get married, if they've had them as single women. It's an asset they bring to the marriage. For Mrs. Kinnick to continue to pay the premiums, not to ask you for the money—"

"I gave her plenty of money. Plenty. I never asked what she did with it. She bought the food, the furniture, anything else we needed."

"And she never told you about the policy?"

"Not once. She never even hinted."

Purcell squinted against the sunlight coming through the display window. He asked, "Why do you think she kept quiet about the policy, Mr. Kinnick?"

"How the—I can't answer that."

"There must have been a reason."

"Look, Midge was always an independent sort of woman. Even after we were married, she insisted that she keep her old friends."

"Men friends, Kinnick?"

"No, of course not. That is—I guess not. She never said, one way or the other. I knew a few of her acquaintances, naturally. Those I knew were women."

"It doesn't seem right, she wouldn't tell you."

"It's too bad you can't dig her up and ask her."

"Maybe even then she wouldn't tell us," Purcell said slowly. "Women are funny creatures. They have unusual reasons for things, sometimes. It just may be that she considered her policy to be an asset she was bringing to the marriage, that she wanted to keep it a secret so that when she paid it up, she could surprise you with it."

Kinnick was suspicious. "It could be that way, yes."

"On the other hand, she could have told you all about it."

Dan glared at him. The investigator shook his head and went on, "I don't suppose we'll ever know, not really."

"Maybe she didn't think it was important," Kinnick muttered.

"Oh, come now, Kinnick. A policy that size is a definite financial asset. She would be aware of its value. I just can't understand why she wouldn't tell you about it. You're sure she didn't, are you?"

Anger was a flame in Dan Kinnick. The patient voice of the adjuster, his constant prodding, his obvious suspicions, began to goad him. If Ben Vardon hadn't stopped by at the cemetery to speak to him about this Purcell, he'd have blown his stack before now. He fought to put a damper on himself.

"Look, Purcell, this policy was as much of a surprise to me as Midge's death. I'm still a little shaky from that. I haven't been sleeping much lately."

"Guilty conscience, Mr. Kinnick?"

Dan took a long step forward, but Purcell never moved. He choked out, "I ought to fire you out on your ear. Let's stop beating around the bush. You think maybe I killed her, is that it? You think I need forty thousand, maybe."

Purcell pounced. "Ah, you know about the double indemnity clause? I thought the policy was a surprise?"

"Ben Vardon told me about that. He told me to hold my temper, too."

"Ah, you have a bad temper. Did you and your wife often quarrel?"

"Look, now—"

"Don't you want to answer that, Kinnick?"

"Yes, I'll answer it. We had our spats, sure. What married couple doesn't? But not lately. Not for a couple of months. Things were going nice and smooth for us."

"Why?"

When Kinnick looked blank, Purcell spread his hands. "A district attorney might ask, were things going so smoothly because you were going to murder her? Was that the reason, Kinnick?"

"By God—"

He stood over the insurance man, his hands balled into big fists. He was trembling, actually trembling with the anger in him. Purcell showed no fear, but rather regarded him with a curious, open-eyed stare.

Purcell said softly, "No need for temper. I'm doing you a favor, really. If it weren't for the man who saw your wife skid, you'd be in a bad spot, Kinnick. That car was always kept in your garage, wasn't it? Nobody but you ever worked on it. Are you sure it was in tiptop shape? If anybody had an opportunity to tamper with it, you did. Nobody would know what you were doing. You could have rigged the car to go out of control, somehow.

"I asked myself all those things about you.

"I went to see Vardon and Young. Young told me he saw her skid, saw the car go through the fence. Vardon told me how much in love the two of you were.

"I had to come see you, anyhow."

Kinnick felt weak, listening. This man was right. He was the only mechanic who ever touched the Century. If there was anything wrong with it, he'd be the only one anybody could blame. Sweat came out on his face. He put a hand in his back pocket for a handkerchief. He wiped his forehead, staring down at the blank-faced Purcell.

"I never looked at it from that angle."

"Only lawyers and insurance adjusters do that. We've been trained to look for the angles, the unsuspected undercurrents."

"I don't need that money. You want to see my bank book? My checking account? I'll be glad to sign a release, some sort of paper saying you can keep the money."

Purcell shook his head. "It isn't that simple. There are laws. Even if we wanted to—which we don't—we couldn't do that. If my report says you're entitled to the money and that there's no need for any further investigation, you get it."

The insurance man was unzipping his briefcase, lifting out some papers. "I'd like you to answer some questions and sign a few forms, Kinnick. I may as well tell you, I'm satisfied it was an accident. I wasn't sure until I'd been to see you face to face, until I'd prodded you the way I did."

Kinnick felt relief slam through his middle, making him weak.

Purcell went on, taking a ballpoint pen from his pocket and making a notation on the topmost paper. "A guilty man would never have reacted the way you did. I pride myself on my knowledge of human character. It's part of my job assets, this ability to know people. If I'm satisfied, the company is satisfied. Unless something else turns up, of course."

"Yeah, sure."

"Now if you'll just answer a few routine questions. . . ."

Kinnick began dropping into the corner tavern for his suppers. He was no cook, never had been. He could fry or boil an egg and some strips of bacon and make good coffee, but he had neither the patience nor the sense of timing that a good cook must have. Twice he tried roasting a juicy eyeround; both times he burned it. He could grill a steak, but steaks got monotonous after a while.

When he finished his meals, he usually went into the barroom and played pool with one of the usual hangers-on for drinks. At first he won, but he was not used to liquor—not the way these day-in-day-out drinkers were —and toward the end of the evening he always lost. After a while, his suppers were costing him anywhere from ten to twenty dollars. It was too high a price to pay for companionship, he decided, but he could not face the empty apartment.

It was Willie Magruder who snapped him out of it.

The dour old Scotchman laid a neatly-wrapped porterhouse on his office desk, five minutes before closing time one night. "Take it home an' cook it, laddie. Stay i' the house tonight. You are no' lookin' so well. You have been makin' mistakes wi' the motors you've been checkin' over. I'm gettin' a wee bit tired o' correcting your errors."

With that, the Scot settled his tweed cap a little more firmly on his white head and went stalking off into the night. For a long time Kinnick sat staring down at the steak. The old man was right, of course; he'd been lost in his own loneliness so long it had become a habit. The time for self-pity was over. Only that morning the check had come from the Aetna: forty thousand dollars, it read. The insurance company was closing its books on Midge Kinnick. It was time for him to do the same.

He put the steak in a paper bag and locked the garage behind him, leaving on a small electric light over the cash register, a habit he'd begun since the night of the break-in. The porterhouse made a good weight in his arm as he walked up the block. He wondered if there were any charcoal briquettes left in the pantry. He and Midge used to charcoal grill their meat a lot during the long summer evenings. He would cook it that way tonight, out in the back yard, wearing his hunting jacket against the cold December air.

The telephone rang when he was pouring his second cup of coffee, close on to eleven o'clock. It was Mrs. Conover from Hamilton Avenue over in the Bayswater Knoll section.

"Dan, can you give me a hand? My battery went dead

and I've got to be in White Plains tomorrow morning at
eight-thirty. I know you've closed up and that you rarely
make night calls, but this is an emergency and—"

"Why sure," he found himself saying. The steak had
been cooked to perfection for a change, and even the
coffee was strong and fragrant. He was feeling right
with the world, in a mood to do a favor. "I'll put a new
battery in the car and buzz right over."

In a way he was glad Mrs. Conover had called. It
would give him something to do. He locked the apartment door behind him and zippered up his red Mackinaw. He had kept so much to himself lately that he'd
had no chance to really test-run the new Holiday he'd
bought the week before. Tonight was as good a time as
any.

He whistled as he drove up Central Park Avenue,
skirting the Thruway. The Olds was purring softly, the
snow tires making a faint hum on the concrete. He
reached for a cigarette, pressing the lighter into its dash-
board slot. The smoke tasted good.

He braked the car to a halt in the Conover driveway, absently noting that the lights were on in the living
room and in an upper bedroom. No need to go to the
door. He could do this without bothering Mrs. Conover.
He unlocked the car trunk, lifted out a new Auto-Lite.
The garage overhead was up. He could see the rear end
of the red Caddy gleaming in his headlamps.

When the battery was installed, he warmed up the
motor, then slid out. Mrs. Conover was at the side door,
beckoning to him.

"Dan, oh, Dan."

Mrs. Conover was a pretty woman in her late thirties
or early forties. She was wearing a black taffeta house-
coat belted about a slim waist, but her hair was carefully
curled and dusted with silver. She was wearing diamond
earrings and evening slippers below blue stockings. She
had everything on but the dress, he figured.

"I want to pay you, Dan," she smiled, holding the door
open. "Brrr, come on in. It's freezing out there."

Her heavily lipsticked mouth flashed a smile at him.
There was green eyeshadow on her eyelids, and a black
beauty patch beside a slim nostril. A good-looker this

Mrs. Conover, even if she had been divorced twice and widowed once. He'd heard she got richer each time. Mrs. Conover and her kind moved in a different world from him.

She stood in the brightly lighted hallway, slippered feet planted firmly apart on the black and white linoleum tilework of the floor, fumbling in her handbag, looking up at him almost flirtatiously.

"Grácious, I can never find my—oh here. Here's my wallet. Now how much do I owe you?"

"I could send a bill, Mrs. Conover."

"No, no. No bill. This is an after-hours' emergency. Just name a price." The wallet was open and he could see half a dozen twenties in her hand.

"Well, the battery is fifteen and—"

She held out two twenties to him, smiling. "Will this cover it?"

He said, "It's too much. I couldn't—" .

"Nonsense. Take it!"

"I'd rather bill—"

She was close and perfumed, and he could smell whisky on her breath. Her long-lashed eyes widened. "For goodness sake, Dan! Are you in business for money or not? You did me a big favor. I want to show I'm grateful."

"Well, if you insist."

He took the money, reminding himself that he could always make up the difference to her in future services. He slid the crisp bills into his worn wallet.

"Thanks, Mrs. Conover. Any time."

He put a hand to his hat and went out into the darkness. He heard the metallic rasp of the bolt sliding home. As he walked across the lawn to his car, he glanced up at the night sky. There was a three-quarter moon, silvery and clear. He picked out Orion and the Big Dipper. It was a fine night, a good night to be alive.

Five minutes later a man was shooting to kill him.

Is this all, Daniel Philip Kinnick? Are there any other threads of your everyday life to be gathered up and bound into a living fabric of memory? Search wide, search deep. The unsuspected lilt of laughter or the glance from narrowed eyes, a handclasp or a word shouted out in anger: each writes its part on the page of life. What man can interpret the casual nod of a stranger or the emotion which causes him to act in anger? No man is a world unto himself.

"I guess that's it," said Kinnick lamely.

"Yeah," said Ben Vardon heavily.

Dawn was coming through the window above the sink. It cast a pale red glow over the wall tiles, over the butter and cream set beside the empty coffee cups. The detective yawned and straightened, rubbing a hand across his stubble-bearded jowls.

Dan spread his hands. "As far as I can tell, there's nothing else. You can see it must have been a mistake, can't you? In all the things I've talked about, I haven't unconvered any reason why anybody'd want me dead."

"If you did, I didn't see it."

A silence grew between them. Upstairs they could hear Kathy moving about, going from her bedroom to the bath and then into one of the children's rooms. The clock over the refrigerator read 6:31. A new day was beginning, a day Dan Kinnick would not have been alive to see except for a misaimed gun in the dark hours of the night.

He stood up. "I've taken up enough of your time, Ben. Maybe you can still get an hour of shuteye."

Ben shook his head. "My job. 'S what a friend is for. Besides, what about yourself? You got to work too. Hell, forget it. This isn't the first time I've spent a sleepless night."

Vardon walked to the front door with him. As he was opening it he asked, "You want me to make out a report on this, Dan? I should, you know."

"Do what you think is right, Ben."

He walked into the dawn, down the Vardon front steps. There was a numbness in him, but that was only normal. It would fade fast enough once he opened the garage and began working. Around three o'clock was when he'd really feel the tiredness. Well, Willie could take over then.

There was nobody to take over for him if those men

made another try for him, though. As he climbed into the Holiday, his middle felt empty and hollow.

He was scared.

Damn scared.

CHAPTER FIVE

Two mornings later, Donna Morrison stepped out of her blue Comet dressed in a pumpkin sweater and charcoal brown skirt. As Dan Kinnick came toward her, he told himself she had never looked more vitally alive, more exciting. Her new maturity gave her an added graciousness, an inner warmth he found oddly comforting.

Excitement built a lazy fire deep inside him. Now that Midge was gone, he could let himself think about this girl who was so much a stranger to him. The guilt which had bothered him when he remembered the October afternoon at the Lodge and the way he'd held Donna in his arms, kissing her, was something out of his past. He need no longer concern himself with loyalty to Midge. His life was changed, now his wife was dead.

"Dan," she smiled, holding out both hands. "You didn't come up to the Lodge, so I came down here and took a motel room." She gave a mock sigh. "The things a girl has to do to get herself a date."

"Dinner and dancing," Dan grinned. "A gabfest like old times."

He wanted to take her in his arms and cover her mouth with kisses. Maybe she could see his need in his eyes because she wrinkled her nose at him and laughed breathlessly. He found his stare drawn again and again to the pushing mounds of her breasts and the gentle slope of her haunches. Donna Morrison was a big girl now, and an entirely different person in his eyes.

They ate at the Washington Arms in Mamaroneck. The

52

roast beef was thick and juicy, and when a muffin girl brought hot buttered garlic bread, Donna broke off two pieces, handing one to him. As he watched her white teeth sink into the delicacy, Dan reflected that the last time he'd dated Donna Morrison, she'd been a schoolgirl. Now she was a mature woman.

Her smooth white shoulders lifted nakedly from a tight black crepe cocktail gown. Thick black hair was piled up in a pouf with Empire curls, giving her a pert, saucy look which highlighted the attractiveness of her faintly slanted eyes and generous red mouth. He had the feeling he had never really known this woman, no matter how familiar he'd been with her during her girlhood.

Slowly, under the insistence of her bright eyes and laughter, the knot within him began to unravel. His inner coldness thawed and he found himself talking freely, without hesitation.

He sketched out the night in Bayswater Knoll when a Cadillac had roared by and a man had taken a shot at him. Nor did he bother to hide the satisfaction he felt when she showed fear for his safety, relishing the haunted look in her eyes and the gentle clasp of her fingers on his own. He told her about the time his garage had been broken into, and the untouched money in his cash register drawer.

She frowned over that, puzzled. "Why would anyone break into your garage and not take the money? Unless—"

He interrupted her, explaining how Ben Vardon had searched the premises, how he and Willie had decided it was the work of teen-agers.

She shook her head. "Not necessarily. Suppose somebody had been trying to kill you even then?"

"Kill me?" he asked blankly.

"Well, it isn't such a farfetched idea," she protested defensively. "You were going to use the car yourself. You told Midge that you had some sort of repair call to make."

"At Hartwell's. That's right."

"So Midge makes you postpone it. She takes the car instead. The accident that happened to her could just as well have happened to you. Maybe it was supposed to."

"I never thought about that. Neither did Vardon."

"It seems clear enough to me. Suppose this man who

wants you dead tried to kill you and make it look like an auto accident. He didn't know, of course—he couldn't know—that your wife would take the car instead of you."

Kinnick scowled. "It makes sense. Somebody breaks into the garage, tampers with the car, fixes it so an accident would happen, maybe not right away, but after I'd been driving for a while."

He paused, considering possibilities. "He could have sawed through the steering wheel—or removed a few lugs from the front wheels—or even tampered with the brake hoses so the fluid would leak. The fluid would remain until the brakes were pumped so as to eject it. It'd be possible to drive quite a distance before the brakes failed, or the steering post snapped, or the front wheels gave way.

"How far anybody'd be able to drive depends on the circumstances, the frequency with which you'd have to use the brakes or the bumps which might break the steering post. It wouldn't happen right away, certainly. Midge could quite easily have driven from the garage to the Ardsley Hill Road without trouble. Then on that steep incline, bearing down on her brakes, always assuming they'd been tampered with—sure! I'll bet that's the way it was. God, I was blind."

Dan shook his head, grinning ruefully. "A hell of a subject for a guy and his girl to be talking about on their big date. Murder methods, yet. Come on, let's liven up the show with dance music and a few drinks. I know a place in Tuckahoe."

Donna sat close to him on the run from Mamaroneck to the little bar and grille, as if she were afraid that, once having found him, she was going to lose him. Remembering the attempts that had been made on his life, Dan thought glumly that she might be right.

The Tuckahoe bar and grille was almost empty. Only three tables in the rear of the tavern held couples. Dim lights shrouded the booths and tiny dance floor. A jukebox standing by a wooden divider was playing muted music. Kinnick ordered rye on the rocks while Donna lifted off her fur jacket.

Then they were clinging, her head resting on his chest, dancing slowly, lost in one another. Her pouffed hair tickled his chin so that he had to scratch it against her temple, making her laugh softly and wriggle closer. Against his chest he could feel her breasts going hard. So she was also feeling this animal need that bothered him. He smiled and held her even tighter.

Nobody paid any attention to them. The other couples were lost in their own companionship and the bartender was a three-hundred pounder who had seen his fill of people in love. The lone man leaning against the bar was lost in a racing form, eyes glued to its printed pages.

In the shadowed privacy of their booth, he pulled Donna against him, bending to find her mouth with his lips. The savagery of her response to his caress both pleased and surprised him. Her lips were moist, loose, then firmed to return the fury of his kiss. After a moment, she began to tremble and pulled free.

"Damn you," she whispered. "Now you've gone and done it. I'll never get to sleep tonight."

"Good. Then we won't go home."

"It'll cost you, mister. Staying out late nights makes me thirsty. You'll have to buy me drinks."

She looked into her compact mirror while the bartender brought them refills. Snapping it shut, she asked the heavy-set man, "Do you believe in love?"

He grinned, "I sure do, lady."

"You got a girl?"

"For thirty years. And three grandchildren."

Donna lifted her glass. "To your girl."

The three-hundred-pound man said, "I don't often treat myself, ma'am, but I'll join that toast. And thank you."

The wall clock read fifteen minutes after four as Kinnick guided Donna across the dance floor and along the bar into the cool night air. She leaned into him heavily, giggling at the pressure of his arm.

"You don't let a girl breathe, darling."

"I don't want to let you go."

"Mmmm," she murmured hazily. "Don't want to be let go."

The drive to her motel took close to an hour. Dan walked her to the door of her room. Under the frosted glass lamp inset in the ceiling, he kissed her and let his hands rove down her back to her sloping hips.

"Dan?"

"Mmmmm?"

"Ought I ask you in?"

"Sure. So I can be a gentleman and refuse the invitation."

"Would you refuse it?"

"Ask me and find out."

"Something tells me I'd better not."

She leaned to kiss him, then whirled and thrust her key into the lock. Kinnick watched the door swing open, heard the click of an electric light switch and saw a small bed and night table, a carpeted floor and a wall tinted powder blue. Donna pursed her lips and blew a kiss, then closed the door gently.

Kinnick wanted to shout his delight to the world.

He contented himself with a sigh and a shake of his head on his way to the Holiday. He drove slowly through the night, down the Saw Mill River Parkway to Yonkers Avenue and then east.

The garage windows glinted in the moonlight as he braked and got out to unlock and lift the overhead door. The scent of perfume filled the car and made him close his eyes and dream a little after he'd run the car inside.

He had left the car and was walking toward his house when the Cadillac turned the corner. It came slowly, at crawling speed, its powerful motor almost silent. Two men sat in the car, men whose faces were shadowed by down-pulled hatbrims.

Kinnick felt his heart surge up into his throat.

His heart choked him, so high up. It pounded so hard it shook his body and he stood frozen watching the car come closer—

He tried to see the license plate, but the car was in the shadows, moving slowly. Kinnick realized suddenly that he made a perfect target on the sidewalk. There was no room for doubt. This was the same car from which a man had taken a shot at him three nights ago.

They were going to kill him now.

He threw himself flat on the sidewalk. The Cadillac picked up speed. Kinnick rolled over. A knee-high stone fence was only a few feet away bordering a lawn. With his muscles bunched, he came to his feet, ran two steps, then made a flying leap. He went over the fence like a diver going into shallow water. He landed on his front and the wind went out of him, but he was safe.

He lay and listened to the Cadillac pick up speed and move off down the street. There was no gunshot. Kinnick lay on the ground and shook.

He ran all the way home.

CHAPTER SIX

His fist hit the desk top at Police Headquarters. Anger was a jumping frustration inside him. His voice was low, but heavy with controlled fury.

"Damn it, Ben. I want a look at that car."

"There's no need, Dan. We went over it with a fine-tooth comb."

Kinnick slumped into the straightbacked chair where he was sitting. He'd been so sure, so positive, after what Donna had suggested last night. The same men who'd been trying to kill him had tried before, by cutting the steering post of the Buick or by removing a few lugs from its front wheels or by fooling around with the brake hoses. It had to be one of those probabilities; nothing else added up. Instead of killing him, they'd killed Midge, though.

He asked heavily, "You didn't find anything?"

"Of course we did. It looked as if the brake hoses had been tampered with, to let the fluid run out." Vardon smiled grimly and held up a hand. "Now don't go off half-cocked. Why do you think that insurance adjuster was on your tail? We found the hoses cut, sure. But they just might have been sliced that way in the fall. Everybody agreed on that. Then we checked your tools. None of them showed any rubber particles, not even on a microscopic examination."

"You were pretty thorough, weren't you?"

The detective spread his hands. "It was my job, Dan."

"I know. I know."

"As I say, we didn't find a damn thing that would positively tie you in as the possible murderer of your wife.

Nothing a smart defense lawyer wouldn't make mince-meat out of. If somebody broke into your garage as you claim—and if that somebody cut the brake hoses—he did a damn good job of cleaning up after him. Which was to be expected, I suppose."

"I don't get it."

"Hell, if he was after you, it wouldn't look so good, would it, if a routine investigation turned up the fact that you appeared to have cut your own hoses. It had to look like an accident. Or at the very least, a non-provable murder. So maybe you were lucky, Dan. All around."

"Lucky, the man says," he exclaimed bitterly.

"For one thing, that you didn't drive the Buick after our friend went to work on it. For another, that he took the trouble to clean up so thoroughly after him."

"I could have done the cutting and the cleaning up."

"Don't think we didn't consider it."

"And?"

Vardon shrugged his powerful shoulders. "No self-respecting district attorney is going into court to get a conviction on a murder charge without some positive proof that you caused the accident. The fact that your tools were clean isn't any kind of proof at all. The intruder may have used his own saw. He was after you, not your wife. If he could have known Midge would take the car, maybe he might have left the tool he used if he brought it himself. Or not cleaned yours when he got through with it."

Kinnick shuddered. "Then the fat would be in the fire."

"It would indeed. Purcell considered all those facts before he went to see you. He told me that even if you did kill her, there'd be no way of proving it by law. Besides —there was always the possibility that the hoses shredded like that because of a flaw in them when the car went over the Ardsley Avenue Hill.

"Experts would have so testified. A smart defense lawyer would have seen to that." Vardon glanced down at his hands, and smiled grimly. "I told Purcell he was all wet. If he brought you to trial, I'd take the stand myself. I told him you loved your wife, that you'd never dream of killing her."

Kinnick wondered what Ben Vardon would say if he knew that his good friend Dan Kinnick had been kissing a girl named Donna Morrison last night and as good as asked her to marry him. Motive. Maybe that was all that had kept Purcell from bellowing bloody murder. If he was in debt or gambled, he might have needed money, but his gas station was doing well, and nobody but a moron kills his wife to get money he doesn't need.

If Ben or the Aetna man knew about Donna, they might add two and two and get five. A man sometimes murders his wife so he can be free to love another woman. It might be all the motivation James Purcell would require.

He wasn't out of danger, yet.

Just because Aetna had given him the forty thousand was no guarantee they looked on him as an innocent man. Could be they were giving him a rope with which to hang himself in their eyes and before a judge and jury.

When a hand touched his shoulder, he realized he was leaning forward on the chair, elbows on his thighs, staring at emptiness. Vardon was standing, looking down at him quizzically.

"Go on home, Dan. Stop brooding."

"Yeah, I guess so."

His hand fumbled for his hat. He managed a wry grin. "I feel like suspect number one, even though I didn't have anything to do with it."

Vardon's hand squeezed his shoulder. "Just don't do anything foolish, Dan. Keep your nose clean."

"Yeah. You bet."

He went out into the cold winter day, sick at heart. A few snowflakes were falling, being blown about by the wind. The gray sky reflected his own gloom, he thought, buttoning his overcoat and bending his head against the wind. Apparently he'd been living in a fool's paradise last night, thinking about marriage to Donna, not knowing how close he stood to disaster.

He fumbled his way into his car and sat for a while staring blindly through the windshield. An emptiness inside him held him in thrall. He lost all feeling as a man, discovering himself to be no more than something tossed this way and that by circumstance. Those men in the Cadillac. The law and the Aetna Insurance outfit, watching and waiting for him to make a mistake, to do something on which they could pin a murder case.

And Donna Morrison. God, he couldn't forget her or the taste of her lips and the feel of her big breasts against him. He wanted her so badly, he ached. She'd said they'd have to wait a while. Maybe now, it would be forever.

His hand turned the ignition key. The motor rumbled into life. No sense brooding like this, though. Worry never helped anything. What he ought to do was go back to the garage, fill gas tanks and study oil gauges, fix flats and put on snow tires.

Instead he drove to a bar on Nepperhan Avenue.

He began to drink, slowly but steadily, without taste for the whisky he was downing, without pleasure. Dan Kinnick was trying only to forget Dan Kinnick and his troubles. After a few hours, he succeeded.

The whisky did not make him drunk. It merely lifted him onto a different plane, from where he could stare down at himself with amused detachment. He saw one man among three billion people on this planet Earth, lost in woe and gloom, sitting hunched over a rye on the rocks—his twelfth? fifteenth?—and staring into the bar mirror at his own reflection. A man afraid to die, a man afraid to live. He was just as good as dead, for all the good his life was doing him.

No Donna Morrison to marry and take to bed, no house to buy to make himself a home, no children to be born to them. The black shadow of the electric chair was over him. And somewhere out there in the world beyond the quiet dimness of this bar was a bullet in a gun, waiting for him.

He pushed away the drink into which he had been staring. From his wallet he lifted out two tens and tossed them on the bar. He moved toward the front door, not heeding the bartender who called after him that he had some change coming.

What good was change to a dead man?

What good was anything?

The cold air made him stand still in sudden shock, aware that the whisky was getting to him, now that he was on his feet and moving. He ought not drive home. His reflexes were dull, lifeless. But he kept going, unlocked the car and managed to slide behind the wheel.

He drove carefully, telling himself not to have a crack-up. Purcell might seize on that as evidence he was hiding a guilty conscience, when all he was, was scared witless. His hands clenched around the wheel, trying to steady the car when the road itself and the buildings on either side were dancing a crazy jig.

Maybe it would be better to crash into another car. End it all. Not have to go through tomorrow and the day after and all the rest of them, wondering and afraid. He shook his head to clear it of the fuzziness. He must stop having thoughts like that. A crash would injure other people, not only himself. He bit down on his lip, summoning up the last shred of will power left in him with which to control the moving car.

Then he was on Yonkers Avenue and the traffic along Nepperhan had fallen behind. Drive past the Ramp, go over the Saw Mill River Parkway, head under the Cross County overpass and—

The driveway was there suddenly, in the darkness and the falling snow. He turned the wheel, knew he was over-shooting the macadam, braked the car. He sat leaning on the wheel, taking deep breaths. Back up, get a new start. Do it over.

Somehow he made it onto the garage apron.

He had no energy to lift the overhead door. He would leave the car here, unlocked and unattended. If the snow covered it, if anybody stole it, the hell with it. He slid out and almost fell.

Have to take it easy, walking up the block. It was hard to stand. If those two men came cruising in their Caddy now, they'd find him easy pickings. He grinned wryly. Save the State a job, that's what they'd be doing. Use a bullet on Dan Kinnick, save an electric bill at Sing Sing.

It was slow going. More than once he came to a dead stop, just to stand, to prevent falling down. He wondered vaguely how many of his neighbors would see him and know that Dan Kinnick was stoned. Maybe they wouldn't blame him, though. Dan Kinnick had a lot to put up with.

His hand brought the house key from his pocket out of

long habit, but he could not control his hand long enough to slide it into the lock. He cursed fretfully, seizing his right hand with his left to hold it steady.

Then the door was opening and a hand reached out.

"You poor dear, come on in."

He tried to focus his eyes. A young woman in a thin silken wrapper with thick black hair piled high on her head in a casual way so that some of it fell down to her shoulders, stood framed in the open door. Thyra Prentice. Of course.

" 'Lo, Thyra," he mumbled.

"Hello, yourself. Here, let me give you a hand."

He was too far gone to shake himself free, managing only to protest that her folks would hear and see him.

"They won't," she promised, closing and bolting the front door. "They aren't home. They went to Nyack to visit relatives."

"That's good. I 'preciate that."

She was stronger than he'd thought, taking his weight with her arm about his middle, guiding him along the hall and up the stairs to his own apartment. Even in his drunken condition he understood from the softness of the flesh pressing into him that the wrapper was all she had on. The wrapper and some kind of musky perfume, and high-heeled shoes.

She brought him into his bedroom and let him sink down onto the coverlets. Then she stood back and regarded him, a faint smile curving her mouth. "No, I guess you can't get your clothes off by yourself. I'll have to do it."

"Don't bother, Thy—"

Her hands were on his overcoat, pulling and tugging, then on his jacket and unbuttoning his shirt. His head felt very heavy, suddenly, too heavy for his neck to support. He let his chin fall forward on his chest, trying to lift his arms and straighten out so she could pull the trousers off his legs.

He never knew when he fell asleep.

Kinnick woke to a faint light coming from the kitchen. He lay a moment, staring ceilingward, head throbbing and mouth dry. He squeezed his eyes, and tried to lift a hand to press his eyeballs against the pain, but his arm was so heavy he had to use force to free it.

Something was weighing it down, something heavy. He turned his head and saw Thyra Prentice asleep on the pillow beside him, pinning his arm. He raised himself to an elbow, staring at her. Had he—

His movement waked her. Her eyes opened slowly, staring at him wonderingly. Then memory returned and she smiled, turning on her back, stretching out her arms and legs. The thin wrapper fell away from her shoulder, baring smooth white skin.

"Thyra, did I—that is, if I—"

"You didn't. You were much too looped to make a pass. Too bad." She turned her head on the pillow and smiled at him. "You have a nice body, Dan. I wouldn't have minded if you had."

He grew uncomfortably aware that he was naked under the covers. She must have undressed him. Groaning, he put his head back on the pillow.

"Black coffee," the girl ordered. "And a cold shower."

"Just let me alone," he said thickly.

"Come on, upsadaisy."

She had her warm hands on him, easing him to a sitting position, then helping swing his legs off the bed. She was laughing, but her cheeks were flushed and her eyes brilliant with excitement. Her parents were gone for the night, he remembered vaguely. Maybe Thyra Prentice had things on her mind. She crawled past him on the bed, stood and yanked him upright.

"In you go," she ordered, turning him toward the bathroom with both palms on his shoulders and pushing. "Nothing like a cold shower to get that pain out of your head. I'll make black coffee."

He yielded to the pressure of her hands, stumbling his way past the chaise longue and into the bathroom. He closed the door behind him, wondering why he bothered.

He stepped into the shower, reaching for the tap.

Ten minutes later he was bent over, letting the ice cold water drum down on his head. The pain was gone and he felt wonderfully alive. When his hand lifted to shut off the valve, the smell of perking coffee came to him. He was hungry, very hungry.

"Hey, Thyra," he called. "As long as you're serving, how about some bacon and eggs?"

"Coming up, Dan."

He toweled himself slowly, wondering about the girl. He ought to send her downstairs to her own place, but he had been lonely for too long a time. Talking to Thyra would be like talking to Midge, in a sense. For the first time in weeks he was not preparing food in his own kitchen. He found a bathrobe and slipped into it.

The crisp bacon and the egg, sunnyside up, were waiting for him. Thyra was pouring coffee from the percolator. She lifted her head as he came through the door, giving him a bright smile.

"Well, you look better," she told him. "Almost human."

"Hey, am I going to eat alone?"

"Just coffee for yours truly. My girlish figure."

"Nothing wrong with your figure."

She turned sideways, patting her rounded belly. Under the thin silk wrapper her breasts stood up big and firm. Her long-lashed eyes were studying him wisely as his gaze ran over her.

"You see?" she asked. "The start of a tummy already. Black coffee has no calories. I'll be satisfied with that. You eat, Dan. You look as if you need it."

He enjoyed her mothering. She fussed over him as Midge never did, buttering his toast, spooning sugar and pouring cream into his coffee, nodding her approval as he finished the last of the egg.

"Didn't eat all day, did you?" she smiled.

"Only a doughnut for breakfast."

"You were pretty far out a while ago. Have many drinks?"

"Too many."

"Sometimes it pays to tie one on. Helps you forget things. And you have a lot to forget." She saw his surprise and nodded. "Oh, I know. But just because she's dead doesn't mean you can forget the things she did."

He asked blankly, "Things she did? What things?"

Thyra flushed in embarrassment. "Me and my big

mouth. Forget I said anything, Dan. Here, let me clean up and—"

His hand went out and caught her wrist, bringing her around the edge of the table. She came willingly enough, but she was still embarrassed and there was a sullen pout on her full mouth. He discovered when she was touching his knee, that the silk wrapper was almost transparent.

"What things?" he asked.

Her shoulder moved petulantly. "Oh—things."

His hands shook her where he still clutched her wrist. "Come on, Thyra. Level with me. If you know something I ought to know, spit it out."

She had turned her head to one side. Now her eyes slanted down at him. "Why should I?"

Dan decided he could get more with honey than vinegar; he drew her closer between his legs until he caught the smell of her musky perfume.

There was enough liquor still in him to make him carefree, almost reckless. This woman was the daughter of his landlord. Fool around with her and he might really get himself in trouble. Just the same, she was damned aggravating, with her body only partially hidden under that silk thing, and her defiant mouth and laughing eyes.

He rose slowly to his feet, looked down at her. She was touching his chest with the tips of her breasts; they felt hard, like dull daggers thrusting at him. Her face was lifted so he could see the heat burning in her.

"What things?" he found himself whispering.

"Going around with that man who came calling."

"What man?"

"I don't know his name. He drives a Triumph."

"What was he like?"

"A big guy. Handsome. At least your wife thought so. I saw her kissing him."

"You're a liar," he cried hoarsely.

She moved closer. Now her thighs and belly touched him gently, excitingly. "Am I?" she wondered softly. "Am I a liar, Dan? Him with his arms around her, his hands on her rear, right in the hall outside your apartment door. I saw them when I was home sick from work one afternoon."

She was telling the truth. As surely as he knew he was standing here with Thyra Prentice in his kitchen, he knew this. His hands came up and rested on her shoulders as if for support. There was a dizziness in him. Through the silk, his fingers began kneading the flesh of her shoulders and upper arms.

"She was no good, this Midge," Thyra said gently.

"She was my wife."

"Being a wife doesn't make a woman good. She's born good or bad. Like me." A touch of bitterness ran on her tongue as she went on, "I'm no good, not that way. It's something inside me, like a flaw. Only I'm honest about it. Maybe that's why I never got married. I could never be faithful to one man. I'd see one I wanted— you, for instance, I've been after you for a long time, Dan, but you never seemed to see me on account of that slut you were keeping—"

His hands flung her from him so that her back slammed hard against the kitchen wall. Dishes jumped on the table. Her thick black hair came uncoiled and fell to her shoulders. Her mouth opened in surprise. She stood with her back against the kitchen wall and from surprise, her mood changed to anger.

"Can't you take the truth? Are you so goddam high and mighty you can't conceive of a woman being unfaithful to you? You bastard. I'm sorry I bothered to sober you up."

She pushed away from the wall, moved to go past him. Suddenly ashamed of his outburst, he reached to catch her by the arm. "Thyra, wait. I'm sorry."

"Let go of me!" she spat, and tried to twist free.

He was strong, very strong, and he held her as easily as he might a child. "I'm going to apologize, Thyra. I want you to listen to me and excuse me. I've been through so much—"

Jeering laughter scratched at his nerves. "You poor martyr. Maybe I don't blame Midge for playing around with somebody else. You probably weren't doing her any good in bed anyhow and that's where it counts most be- tween a man and a woman, even his wife. You left her hungry for some real loving. You—"

A muscle jumped spasmodically in his jaw. The liquor

was pounding thickly through his veins like distant drums
beating an erotic message. Who the hell was this bitch
to question his manhood? His fingers tightened on her
arm, and when she winced with the pain of it, pleasure
ran along his nerves.

He might have let her go, even then. But Thyra raised
her eyebrows and asked, "Could you? Could you do it
with her? Or did she really have to go out looking for
it from the man with the Triumph?"

"You tramp," he whispered and yanked her against
him.

She fought, lips drawn back to show white teeth and
red tongue, small fists pounding at his shoulders. Twice
her knee came up, blocked by his shifting thigh. She
tried to bite him, mouth wide open, even as she sobbed
gutter obscenities. His fingers tangled in her hanging
black hair, then he dragged her head backward until
she was looking upside down at the kitchen doorway.
There was a change in the tone of her voice. She still
whispered the obscenities, but now she said them
tenderly, as if to whip him into an erotic frenzy. Her
hips began to move caressingly around and around in
tiny circles.

"Maybe she didn't have to—go anywhere else. Maybe
—she only did it because it was—goddamned exciting
and let her live through the boring times—in between."

"And maybe she didn't do it at all."

"Goddam you. How can you go on talking when—"

His hand brought her head up slowly. Wildness stared
out of her dark eyes as her mouth came open to his
kiss. Tongue flickering, she lunged upward, her arms
going around him like clamps. She was shaking crazily,
moaning deep in her throat, urging her breasts and belly
against him in a sensual rhythm.

Dan Kinnick knew he had to prove himself to this
woman. There was some need deeper than mere satisfaction involved. He almost felt as if he were on trial.
His fingers caught the wrapper, tore it down the back.

Midge was dead.

Donna was far away at the Lodge.

Only this sobbing girl was real. Only this kitchen
where they stood locked in frenzy was real, the only

section of the world that mattered to Dan Kinnick right now. He lifted her, felt her thighs wrap around him and her arms tighten.

Like that, he carried her into the bedroom.

CHAPTER SEVEN

Dawn was in the air beyond the bedroom windows when he rolled away from Thyra to stare upward unseeingly at the ceiling. For the first time in months, he felt relaxed and without nerves, as if he had drained himself of every worry, every fear. He had been not so much a man as an automaton. There had been almost as much rage in him as there had been lust.

After a long time the woman whispered, "Oh, God."

He said dully, still looking at the ceiling, "I suppose you hate me. I wouldn't blame you."

"Hate you? Oh, honey."

Her arm lifted to fall limply across his chest. "Just give me time to catch my breath, Dan. Then I want to apologize myself."

He lifted his head to look at her. She lay with her head pillowed on her left cheek, her black hair spread out behind her. A lazy smile touched her full mouth and there was gratitude in her dark eyes.

"Apologize?"

"For doubting your manhood. Midge was even more of a slut than I imagined. No—wait. Don't get mad. Just listen."

"I'm not mad. I don't have the energy to be mad."

"My mother told me first, said there was a man calling for your wife in the early afternoons. A big man in expensive clothes who drove a sports car. At first I didn't think anything of it. Then I got sick, like I said. I saw them kissing in the hall. They went into the apartment.

"I gave them half an hour. Then I went up to bring

70

back a bag of sugar I'd borrowed. Midge came to the door in a negligee, the thin black one hanging in your closet. Oh, yes. I looked for it while you were sleeping off your drunk. He was still here. At least, his car was parked down the block. And I smelled cigar smoke."

There was a silence between them. Dan realized suddenly that what he was learning made no difference to him. There was no pride left in him, no anger. This girl had done a good job. He was empty of everything but the sense of hearing.

After a moment she went on. "Moms used to see them meet after that day, from time to time during November. Midge would get dressed to the teeth and walk down the block. The man and his Triumph would be there waiting.

"And that night you came home and she wasn't here —you remember?"

He nodded lazily. "She said she'd been with Mabel Hunter."

"She was with him. I saw her go out myself. She met him on Yonkers Avenue. My date called for me after she left. We drove past while she was getting in his car."

His wife playing around with another man, keeping dates on the sly with him. Where had this faceless unknown taken her? To a motel room? To his own home or apartment? She'd gone willingly enough, if he could believe Thyra Prentice. And there was no reason why he shouldn't believe her. She had no axe of her own to grind.

"I wonder who he was?"

"A big man, I told you. Wore expensive clothes."

"And he drove a Triumph."

"A red one."

What difference did the color of a car make when a man learned that his wife had been unfaithful to him? Red. Black. Brown. Green. White. Even two-tone. These were only words cloaking the raw fact of adultery in a bed somewhere, and the grappling of naked bodies in spasmodic, illicit pleasure. Kinnick felt a quick nausea, trying to drive from his mind the way Midge had been when she and he had been together, the rolling of her head back and forth on a pillow, the open mouth, the soft flesh straining toward fulfillment.

He ought to curse or cry, react in some manner. The thought came to him that if Midge had been unfaithful, she deserved neither oath nor tear.

Thyra slid to the side of the bed, peering at the electric clock on the night table. "Seven-ten," she yawned, both arms above her head. "Time to go face the boring, humdrum world." She leaned forward, picking up the torn wrapper, holding it high for his inspection.

"I can hardly walk out in what's left of this, lover."

"Take a ten from my wallet," he told her. "Buy another."

She hesitated, thrusting her bare feet into high-heeled shoes, then looked down at him dubiously. "You have a couple in the closet that belonged to Midge. If I could borrow one?"

"Borrow one? Hell, take them all."

"The black number, for instance. I got a boy friend who positively drools over black chiffon."

She walked with jouncing buttocks to the closet door, slid it back and reached in for the chiffon nothingness trimmed with lace. The shoes gave her pale white legs an extra shapeliness. She was temptation in black mist posing in front of the vanity mirror, turning this way and that before the glass.

He decided he liked Thyra Prentice. She was so goddamn out and out amoral, so honestly hungry for sensation, not hiding it or making it anything other than it was, just a happy romp between two healthy people. She never looked for hidden motives, for a declaration of love or marriage. He wondered if her boy friends appreciated what they had in her. Probably not, the male animal being what he was.

Well, he appreciated her and what she had done for him. "Take anything you want, Thyra. Negligees. Dresses. If you will, even the underwear."

She arched her thin brows. "Sure you won't mind?"

"Hell, I'll never wear them."

"No, that's for sure."

She came to the bed, walking sexily. "I'm grateful, Dan."

He laughed and held up both hands. "You'll kill me, woman. Go away for a while. Give a guy a break."

She looked worried. "Any time, honey. You know what I mean?"

He lay there as she went out into the hall and closed the door behind her. Maybe life wouldn't be quite so complex for him with Thyra living a staircase below. He dozed for a while, a faint smile on his lips.

He woke toward ten and remembered what she'd told him about Midge. He wondered if she'd made all that up about the man in the red Triumph. Hell, there was one way to find out about one of those times, anyhow.

Kinnick padded to the telephone, dialed a Hartsdale number. A woman answered. "Hello? Who is it?"

"Mabe? It's Dan Kinnick."

"Dan? Oh, Dan—how are you? Mamma and I often speak of you and—and Midge. We were so sorry for you. But we told you all that at the funeral parlor."

"I know. I just got to thinking about Midge and— well, I wanted to thank you for the flowers. I've been a little behind in my acknowledgments."

"No need for that. You know how we felt."

"Sure, she felt the same about you. That time you and she went to the movies in November, for instance."

"You must have it wrong, Dan. Why, Midge and I haven't seen each other in over a year."

"Oh? Well, maybe I'm wrong."

"I used to call her, though. Sometimes she was home, more often she wasn't. I guess you two were stepping out."

"Yeah, I guess so."

He hadn't been out with Midge for such a long time, he'd forgotten what it was like. He was always too busy making the gas station pay off. He talked a few minutes more, promised to drop by some afternoon for a chat, and hung up.

His hand clenched tightly around the telephone until his knuckles showed white. Chalk one up for Thyra. Midge hadn't been out with Mabel Hunter that night she claimed she had. Instead, she'd been laying the guy in the red Triumph. The nausea came back to him, stronger than ever.

It took him half an hour to dress, his hands were so clumsy. From time to time he found himself sitting on the edge of the bed, just staring dazedly at the room. Maybe the man in the red Triumph was responsible for the attempts on his life. It just might be that Midge and the man decided to put him out of the way so they could get married.

But no, that made no sense. Wives didn't bother killing their husbands these days to be free of a marriage. Getting a divorce was too easy.

No, there was no connection.

Midge had been playing around. Unfortunately for her, she'd skidded on an icy strip and gone over the edge. It was as simple as that, where Midge was concerned. Had she been on her way to meet him?

Fool. Cuckold. Go look at the horns on your head, in the mirror where Thyra Prentice had been posing. Or now that Midge was dead, maybe the horns were gone, too.

He made coffee and drank it black.

Then he walked to work.

It was a Saturday, and business was good. Cars came and went. The gas pumps were running almost constantly, the oil cans being emptied. He and Willie Magruder found time to squeeze in a brake-lining job and an engine tune-up before noon; but the afternoon was so busy, they didn't get to a scheduled car lubrication until close to five.

Kinnick was standing in the pit with the grease-gun in his hands when Willie roused him from his reverie.

"Mon, ye're worse nor a beginner wi' that thing. Gi'e it here."

"What?" he asked.

"The grease-gun. You've wasted ten minutes joost standin' there. I timed you on my Ingersol. You delayed me long enough on the brake-linin' job, so if ye dinna mind—"

Willie scuttled around under the pit. In three minutes he was done. As he handed back the grease-gun he said, "Why don't you take a little vacation, Dan Kinnick? The gude Lord knows you could use one."

"A vacation?"

Willie explained slowly. Dan had made five mistakes at the cash register, overpaying two and underpaying three customers by noon. After that, Willie ran to get the money, his Scots soul bristling in horror. This took him away from his own chores, he pointed out. The brake-lining job lasted two and a half hours, more than double what it should. Something was bothering Dan Kinnick. The best thing for him to do was go away, so at least he wouldn't be in Willie Magruder's way.

Kinnick went into the little office and sat at the desk, resting his elbows on the advertisement posters and bulletins that had come in the mail. The old Scot was right. He'd been all thumbs today. He'd done more harm than good. Customers didn't relish a glum face with their gasoline. Usually he whistled, exchanging witticisms with the men, gently teasing the married women, handing out penny lollipops to the children.

Right now, Dan Kinnick was a sourpuss.

"Ye'll be makin' bad will, an' that's no lie," Willie grumbled.

Dan smiled wryly. "Maybe you're right, Willie. Maybe I ought to get away from everything."

"What about that girl who was here, some weeks ago?"

"Donna?"

"Aye, that's her name."

The Lodge. Sure, that might be the answer. A week of tramping through the woods—the hunting season was long over, but fresh air never hurt a man—and he would look at life a little differently. A man could think out his problems in the woods. Or at the very least, find a sort of peace. Having Donna beside him would be an extra bonus.

Willie was saying, "Shc mought be gude fer ye, a lass like that. Go dancin' wi' her. Let her make you laugh. A laugh would do you a world of gude."

Not only a laugh, but a rest from the constant anticipation of seeing a revolver thrust into his face and fired. "Willie," he said suddenly, "Willie, if I do go on this vacation, will you promise not to tell anybody—nobody at all—where I am?"

Willie only snorted and moved away.

The cloud lifted from him at that moment. When the

hose rang, he went out to the waiting Ford whistling a little tune. Mrs. O'Malley smiled as she fumbled in her purse.

"You're looking better, Dan. More lively. I'm glad."

"Thanks, ma'am. I feel a little livelier."

And he did. Anticipation was a medicine inside him chasing away the blues, the dispiritedness. The woods around Indian Head would be bare and lifeless at this time of year, but he wanted solitude, actually needed it, as a thirsty man needed water, so he could think things out. He would walk and walk, and sit on a fallen log and whittle for hours on end. The fresh air would be a tonic for his lungs. A part of him knew that Donna Morrison would be even better than all the walking he might do and all the fresh air he might inhale.

He left Willie at the station and hurried through the January darkness toward his apartment, knowing just what he would pack in the four-suiter valise which had been Midge's birthday present to him last year. No suits, except the plain gray flannel, in case Donna wanted to go dancing. Just a couple of sport shirts and his red flannel for outdoor wear. The corduroy trousers, two pairs of slacks, African boots for hiking, the gray suede and the brown leather loafers for taking it easy indoors.

He chuckled. Maybe he'd even get to pose for Donna.

There was movement behind the closed door of the Prentices. Father and Mother Prentice home from Nyack? Or Thyra getting ready for a date with one of her young men? He sighed, remembering last night.

He mounted the steps quietly, aware that he dreaded seeing Thyra walk out into the hall and come after him. He wanted to hit the road fast, eat along the way and reach the Lodge before midnight. Thyra would only upset his plans.

The apartment was dark. Switching on lights he went from the closet to the bureau drawers, lifting out what he needed, folding shirts and inserting slacks on hangers. From the kitchen closet shelf he drew down the valise and tossed it on the bed. It took him half an hour to fill it. Even then, he found himself wondering if he'd packed everything he needed.

He went out, closing and locking the door behind him. He tiptoed down the stairs.

Willie was still at the garage when he backed the hard-top out onto the apron and checked it for gas, oil and water. Unlocking its trunk, he threw in his suitcase. Then he went to the cash drawer and counted out a hundred dollars in fives and tens, and tucked a check for a hundred and fifty, which he'd cashed for one of his neighbors, into his wallet.

"You can keep the rest for tomorrow, Willie. Oh, and take an extra sawbuck for this week and next. Maybe it'll help you forget how much trouble I've been to you lately."

"I willna deny it'll help," Willie nodded, eyes twinkling. "An' forget me an' the garage, ye ken? We'll be here when you return."

"And both the better for my absence."

Willie scratched his unshaved chin and looked wise. "Maybe. Maybe not. Joost be sure to ha'e a gude time."

"I weel that," Dan grinned.

He drove up Yonkers Avenue, turning left onto Central Park Avenue, swinging onto the Thruway just before Mile Square Road. He let the Holiday ease up to sixty, holding it there until the toll bridge before Ardsley, then gunning it back to the mile-a-minute pace. He drove easily, without tension.

The miles slipped away in a hum of tires.

He left the Thruway at Catskill, moving onto 23. It was close to ten, now, and hunger was gnawing in him. He pondered the advisibility of eating at a diner. In less than an hour he'd be pulling into the Lodge parking lot.

Eat or wait? Heads or tails? By the time he could decide one way or the other, the Olds was moving through Tannersville and it was silly to think of stopping.

From three miles away he saw the lights of the Lodge. There seemed to be a lot of them for such a dead season, almost as if there were a party going on. When he slid between the stone gateposts, he found three police cars in the lot and half a dozen uniformed officers on the front porch talking to Pops Morrison. They all turned to look his way.

Pops came down two steps, squinting through the darkness at him. He stared for a few moments, then yelled, "Danny boy! Hey, there. Come over here, son."

He left his bag in the car trunk and met Pops with outstretched hand. Caleb Morrison was in his late forties, big and spare of limb and shoulder. His black hair grayed at the temples, and his face seemed made of smooth brown leather, so weatherbeaten it was. Against that dark skin his small gray mustache appeared almost white.

"Anything wrong?" Dan wondered.

"We found a dead man in the woods day before yesterday," Pops told him. "He'd been dead quite some time. Couple of months, to be exact. The heavy snows covered him."

"A hunter?"

"As near as we can make out. His name's Trubo. Max Trubo. Came up here last October, stayed for a week. Paid in advance. Never noticed when he checked out. Didn't find his things, I know that. Police Chief Andrews has been asking questions. Come on over and meet him."

Andrews was a small man, chunky and hard. His eyes were dark blue and very steady. He was all business. "Don't suppose you knew him, Kinnick?"

"Never heard of him," Dan said. Then asked, "Where'd you find him?"

It was Pops who answered. "Where those wild lilacs grow. You and Donna used to have a name for that part of the trail when you were kids."

"Yeah, I remember. Lilac Lane. We had a lot of names for different parts of those woods. It's too damn bad. I'm sorry. If there's anything I can do, I'll be glad to help."

Andrews growled. "Not much anybody can do. We've got to start backtracking, see what we can learn about him. He wasn't robbed. Had more'n three hundred bucks in his wallet. Odd that we haven't heard about him as a missing person. He can't have a family."

"Funny no animals found him before you did."

"Oh, not so funny. We don't have any scavengers in

this neck of the woods. The deer and foxes wouldn't bother the body."

"No, I suppose not." Kinnick smiled at Pops. "I'm up here for a vacation. No hunting, no fishing, just walking around in the woods, eating three squares a day and sleeping eight, ten hours a night."

One of the policemen grinned. "It's a cinch you won't find anything more exciting than that. Place is pretty dull until late spring."

"Oh, I don't know. I've already run into a police investigation."

They all laughed. Andrews shook hands as he started down the steps. His men went after him, nodding and smiling. Dan waited with Pops until the last car disappeared down the dark country road.

"Donna around?" he asked then.

"In her studio, working hard. Go drag her down, Dan. I don't get to see much of my daughter any more, what with her teaching days and then painting all hours of the night. I'll make the drinks."

"Oh, and Pops, I haven't had dinner."

The older man nodded. "Steak on the coals? Tossed salad? Garlic bread?"

"Hold the garlic bread until I see if Donna's hungry."

Morrison chuckled and moved on up the steps and across the porch into the big room of the Lodge. Dan turned and stared at the brightly lighted barn. His heart was hammering as it hadn't hammered in a long time, and Dan wondered if this feeling was what all the songs were written about, and the books, the movies and the plays. It had never entered into his marriage, and he wondered if this was the element that had been missing between him and Midge, right from the beginning.

She was standing in a pool of lamplight, wearing dungarees and a soiled T-shirt when he opened the barn door. A brush was clamped between her teeth and she was scowling at the canvas where a partly finished still life oil glistened. Her hair was caught up in a ponytail. She lifted the palette in her left hand and took the brush out of her mouth with the right.

Kinnick stood and stared.

She was a little girl in this moment, the one he'd

known so long ago. And yet she was more than that, for her body was mature and rounded, exciting to his eyes as she moved, touching the brush to the canvas. There was a hint of the maternal in her manner, too.

He yelled, "Hey, what gives around here? Where can a guy get some service?"

She jumped, the brush making a wide red sweep across the canvas. "Oh, damn," she snapped, and turned to glare. "Look, mister. The lodge is—Danny!"

She came running, palette and brush forgotten in her hands. It seemed to Dan Kinnick that all his world was running toward him, arms spread wide to embrace him. He caught her, swung her high and kissed her hungrily.

"Dan, oh what a wonderful surprise. I'm so glad to see you." Her fingers tightened on his shoulders. "Nothing wrong, is there?"

"Only my lack of attention at work, according to Willie. He thought I needed a vacation. I agreed with him, so I came up here to spend a week tramping the woods, just loafing."

"It's wonderful, wonderful."

She hugged him tighter, and he realized that Donna wore no bra beneath the T-shirt. As if she sensed his discovery, she drew away, nose wrinkled and eyes laughing. "We live a lazy life up here, Dan Kinnick. Besides, I wasn't expecting company."

"I like it, I like it," he protested.

"Oh, you. Did you see Pops?"

"I did, and ordered steak. He's also making drinks."

"Good. We'll celebrate."

She cleaned her brushes while he admired the still life. She had a good, strong touch, he thought; she made the canvas come alive to his eyes. When he told her this, she shook her head.

"I'm a journeyman painter, no more. I know my limitations." Amusement made her mouth curl. "But it passes the time and keeps me from thinking about you too much."

"Hah! Is that so bad?"

"Only frustrating."

He put his hand on the back of her neck, kneading the soft flesh with his fingertips. She watched him steadily, smiling faintly. "Donna, you know I want to marry you."

"Do I?"

"But I won't marry you until this trouble I'm in is cleared up. No sense making you wife and widow in the same year."

Anxiety forced her to put her arms around him. "It happened again, didn't it? Somebody tried to kill you since I saw you last."

"That same night, on my way home."

He told her about it while she pressed against him, trembling. "Dan—why? Why does somebody want you dead?"

"I don't know, Donna. I just don't."

Her voice was wistful. "I wish you felt you could trust me enough to tell me. Is it over a girl?"

His grin reassured her. "No, nor gambling debts, nor mobsters, nor any other reason I can think of, unless it's a case of mistaken identity. But I can't buy that. One try at killing me, yes. Not two or three."

Her eyes were frightened for him. "There has to be a reason. Only a madman goes around trying to kill somebody without a reason."

"Those men in the Caddy were no madmen." He shrugged. "I came up here to forget my troubles. Let's go find Pops."

They walked hand in hand from the studio.

It was after ten in the morning when he woke to stare around him at the big room with its maple furniture and flintlock rifle on a rack over the red brick fireplace. Dan came up on an elbow before he remembered and sank back into the covers, stretching, feeling his body quiver with vitality. The sun was golden warmth flooding through the windows, bathing the quilt rugs on the floor.

"Flapjacks," he said softly, "with sausages and maple syrup."

And later in the day, Donna would meet him beyond Indian Rock, after he'd had his fill of tramping the woods, and drive him home for dinner. Afterward, they would go dancing. He began to dress with anticipation strong inside him.

When he was through with breakfast, Pops put a thermos bottle and a bag of sandwiches on the table. "To make sure you don't starve to death."

Dan looked up. "The guy they found in the woods. I don't suppose he starved to death?"

"Rifle bullet—right between the eyes."

"Hunting accident."

"First one we've ever had here," Pops said heavily. "Oh, I know they happen. After all, when you give out fourteen million hunting licenses a year—which is the figure, roughly—you've got to expect to find some nuts using them. Year or so ago, there were over three hundred men killed in hunting accidents. Close to two thousand accidents, all told, with gunshot wounds that weren't fatal added in."

"You've made a study of it."

"I did some years back, when I started insisting that my boarders take safety measures. Some states don't even list hunting deaths, so maybe my three hundred figure is a little small."

"I always wear a red shirt or Mackinaw."

Pops smiled grimly. "That's no surefire way of keeping safe. Lots of men get killed wearing some of the brightest damn red jackets you ever saw. Trouble is, they give hunting licenses in some states to kids under sixteen. A damn fool stunt. It's the young ones do most of the fatal shooting. Inexperience, I suppose. Excitement. They shoot first and look after."

"Think a youngster did it?"

"If he did, he didn't come from the Lodge. I don't let fool kids go hunting on my land. Chief Andrews knows that, knows I make my hunters take every precaution possible." He shrugged. "I can't patrol the place. No telling when somebody parks his car on the edge of the road and takes a rifle into the woods."

Dan looked thoughtful. "You know, it would be easy to get rid of a man by way of a hunting accident. It would be hard as hell to prove first degree murder, or even manslaughter."

"It would. In one state there were only twenty criminal prosecutions out of over three hundred hunting deaths. Juries go easy in cases like that. In the woods it's easy to make a mistake. A guy wants a deer. He sees something move. Up comes his gun. He squeezes the trigger. Result, no deer, only a dead man. New York's made it criminal negligence with a fine of a thousand bucks or five years in jail if there's a hunting accident. Funny. I've seen men change their complete personalities as soon as they get a gun in their hands. Must bring out the savage in them."

"Well, hunting's big business. Where money's involved, people are inclined to blink an eye."

"I guess that explains it, partly. Then there's buck fever, that'll make a man freeze on target, or get so jittery he shoots at any damn thing that isn't nailed down. I try to keep men like that away from the Lodge, Dan. I thought I'd succeeded pretty well at it, until now."

Kinnick shook his head. "You can't blame yourself, Pops. Anybody could have shot the man. As you said, somebody with a rifle and a car parked on the side of the road."

Pops smiled faintly. "I know. It doesn't make me feel any better, though. I saw the man when they brought him out. He wasn't pretty, not at all."

"I'll be extra careful today."

"Oh, you won't have any trouble, now the hunting season's over. It's only during the fall and early winter you have to watch out."

"What about small game? The season on raccoons and rabbits lasts right through February."

Morrison rubbed his jaw thoughtfully. "Maybe you'd better walk careful, at that. Might be somebody from town out for a shot or two. You got your jacket?"

"And a red hat," Dan grinned. "And a knapsack of sorts to carry my lunch in."

"Take along a gun, Dan. You might see a hare."

It was on the tip of his tongue to refuse, but he remembered the men in the Cadillac and decided that if, by some trick of the devil, they'd traced him up to the Lodge, he wouldn't be absolutely helpless. "I'll borrow that Marlin .22, Pops, if you don't mind. And give me a hatful of solid-point bullets, just in case I run into something edible."

The air was cold and crisp. The occasional gusts of wind made moaning sounds as they ran between the bare branches of the white oaks and along the scattered rocks and windfalls. The sky was leaden overhead; it looked like another snow. Not that he minded, might be fun to try his hand at snow shoes again. If they closed the schools, Donna could come with him.

Snow still lay in the more thickly wooded areas, back from the narrow footpath where Kinnick walked. Here and there thin twigs and barren stems thrust upward from their white covering, and big boulders, warmed by the sun, bulked gray and stark against the dark boles. He let his eyes roam, feeling the lure of these wild places, as he had all his life.

A man was half-dead, back in the city. Only here under a heavy sky and with the fresh air scented with loam and cool with coming snow, did he really feel alive. A tingle ran along his bloodstream. His every step made him appreciate the sweetness of life, even while it caused him to remember how near death had come to him.

His gaze searched the rolling woodlands falling away below as he came to the crown of a hill. A big jackrabbit scampered from the underbrush twenty yards away, bounding for the safety of a rockpile. Dan watched it go, feeling the weight of the Marlin Mountie over his forearm, but ignoring it. The rifle was not for hunting today, but protection. He went on looking down at the forest, holding his stare, knowing that if anything moved he would be aware of it.

There was nothing, only the empty woodlands and the air blowing past his face. A glance at his wrist watch showed the time to be twenty minutes past one. He'd been walking for three hours. Time he was hunting a place to eat the sandwiches Pops had prepared.

He found a flat rock on a grassy knoll and sat there, munching slowly, savoring the roast beef and home-baked bread, the coffee warm from the thermos. He took his time, enjoying the day and his unaccustomed laziness. By God, he'd do this a lot more often from now on. Get away from Yonkers for a few days, tramp the woods, eat out in the open like this. Made a man feel on top of the world. Out here under the sky, his problems seemed to belong to somebody he didn't know.

Dan chuckled, reaching into the Mackinaw for an Old Gold. He struck a match, inhaling deeply, letting the smoke swirl out through his nostrils. With practiced hands he folded the waxed sandwich wrappings, tucked them into the paper bag and placed it inside the flattened knapsack.

He poured the rest of the coffee into the tin cup and sipped it slowly while he finished his cigarette. Ought to be a law compelling a man to get away from his work and daily routine once every few months. You worked so hard you sometimes forgot there was anything other than the same old day in day out grubbing for a dollar or a five-spot.

Carefully, he crushed out the cigarette and lay back on the flat stone, hands behind his head, watching the sky. He thought about Donna and what kind of wife she'd make him, if he lived so long.

If those men in the Caddy let him live.

CHAPTER EIGHT

The snow began during dinner, while they were finishing dessert.

Donna went to the window, lifting back the drapes and staring out into the darkness at the falling white flakes which were as large as cotton puffs. The ground was covered completely even at this early hour and the snow gave no signs of stopping. Donna turned and regarded Dan impishly.

"I didn't want to go dancing anyhow," she smiled. "Now I can do what I've always wanted."

"What's that?" wondered her father, spooning sugar into his cup.

"Do an oil of Danny."

Kinnick protested, but without conviction. Within minutes, in borrowed boots, he was running through the snow with Donna toward the barn.

While she threw off her parka and shook snow from her hair, he built up the fire in the studio hearth. When he had it blazing he turned to find her setting up a new canvas on the easel, bringing her paint table and brushes from the shadows.

"Just sit down anywhere, Danny boy. Throw off your jacket and loosen your shirt collar." She turned and presented her back, smiling over a shoulder. "Then you can unzip me."

"Unzip you?"

"I can't work all dressed up. I have to be comfortable." She wriggled her buttocks at him. "Come on, hurry up. I'm anxious to start work."

He ran the zipper down to her black lace panties. Her

back was smooth and white. Dan bent and kissed her. Donna shivered.

"You'd better cut that out, Dan Kinnick," she said with a wry laugh. "You'll get me out of my working mood. Help yourself to a cigarette while you're waiting." She gestured to a cigarette box on the coffee table before the big couch.

The box was empty. "You might know," grinned Dan, and fumbled in the pocket of his Mackinaw where it lay across a chairback, bringing out his silver case and snapping it open. He held out the case to her.

"Have one of mine. After all, you sent the case back to me."

"I remember. I gave it to that man from White Plains. He said he knew you. Oh, what was his name?"

"Jackson? Fred Jackson?"

"That's right. He drove a red sports car. A Triumph."

Dan felt his insides turning over. His hand tightened on the cigarette case until the knuckles whitened. "A Triumph? A red Triumph?"

She stared at him. "What's wrong, Dan?"

He said dully, "Midge was seeing a man who drove a red Triumph all during November. She had him in the apartment and God knows where else. Maybe in his place, maybe in some motel room. I never knew who he was, except that he drove a red Triumph."

"You aren't sure it's the same man, though? Jackson, I mean."

"No, certainly not. Maybe I ought to go see him."

Donna put her hand on his shoulder. "Please don't, Dan. I don't like that man. I never should have given him your cigarette case, but he said he lived near you and—well, I had no reason not to."

"Hell, it's probably a coincidence. There's more than one red Triumph in the world. Just the same I want to see him face to face, talk to him."

"You'll lose your head, start a fight."

"No, I won't. I promise. No fight. No angry words, even." He considered that, head tilted slightly. "It'll be like closing a book after you've read it, or putting a period at the end of a sentence. To put an end to my years with Midge, maybe. I can't explain it. It's just a feeling I have."

He was surprised to find there was no bitterness, no hatred in him toward Jackson. He hadn't cottoned to him when he'd first met him; but even now, even if he had been playing around with Midge—and instinctively Dan felt sure he had—he felt no special animosity toward the man. It was over and done with. Midge was dead. He would let her rest in peace. But by seeing Jackson he would be burying her in a special way, putting her forever out of his mind.

Donna brushed her hands together. "I've lost my mood," she said somberly. "I don't feel like painting any more." She came into his arms and pressed her softness close. "Dan, I'll die if anything happens to you."

The snow stopped falling in the middle of the following forenoon. The high school where Donna taught art was closed until the plows could get through to clear the main roads. They went skiing on the slopes beyond the Lodge and staged a snowball fight with Pops and Johnny Anson. They built a snowman in the empty parking lot and drank hot buttered rum before the main fireplace in the Lodge living room.

These were days which Dan knew would never come again. Never could they duplicate the bittersweet aliveness. It was as if they played together on the edge of a yawning chasm, knowing one misstep would plunge them into disaster. The knowledge made every sight and sound and taste that much sweeter.

Then it was time for Dan to say good-by. Donna said her farewells in her barn studio where she could sniffle and blow her nose without Pops looking on. She made him promise to come up soon and threatened to come down for him if he stayed away.

Dan drove homeward slowly, the sense of loss strong within him. The week had been far more than he had anticipated. It was as if he were refreshed by long sleep.

He could face those men in the Cadillac now when they came to find him. He would buy a gun himself; Ben Vardon would see that he got a permit; and next time he was shot at, he would fire back. Maybe that was his whole trouble. He was a sitting duck for a killer. Just as any other man would be who had no weapon for his own defense.

It was after midnight when he pulled the Holiday into the garage, removed his four-suiter from the car trunk and locked the overhead doors behind him. He walked swiftly, wondering if the Caddy would swing around the corner on him.

He met no one.

His key slid into the front door lock easily. The lights were out in the Prentices' downstairs apartment. He went up the staircase, being careful to make no noise. He unlocked his door and switched on the wall lights.

Carrying his valise into the bedroom, he tossed it on the covers.

And the bed blew up in his face.

CHAPTER NINE

There was a blossoming redness in his eyes and a deafening roar at his ears. His valise went up into the air and the four-poster shook apart in a spray of torn bedding and splintering wood. The shock wave was like a giant fist ramming against his chest, driving him backward off his feet and dropping him onto his back.

He lay there, feeling only a terrible numbness.

Dead. The bastards did it. They got me at last. A bomb on my bed. If I hadn't tossed the valise onto it—

His eyes stared wide on blackness.

Later on there was pain.

His eyes opened, his lids feeling very heavy. He stared at a white ceiling and part of a papered wall. His head turned slowly. This was a small bedroom, belonging to a woman. He frowned. His head turned the other way and now he saw an open door and heard voices.

"Hey," he yelled weakly.

Quick footsteps running and then Thyra Prentice was through the doorway smiling down at him, a hand coming out to pat his hand where it lay on the coverlet. She was wearing a wrap-around robe and pajamas. Right on her heels came Ben Vardon, a little gray around the eyes. Thyra's father and mother stood in the open doorway and stared at him. There was fear on both their faces.

Ben said, "A doctor's been here and gone, Dan. How are you?"

He stirred his legs and wriggled his hips. The pain was

dull now, mostly a slow ache running all through him. Remembering the explosion, he tried to sit up.

Thyra put a hand to his chest and pushed him down again. When he caught her eyes he saw worry mixed with amusement, and he knew that he was lying in her bed.

"I guess I'm all right. What happened?"

"Don't you know?" asked Ben.

"Well, in a way. I came back from a week's vacation. I went into the bedroom. I threw my valise on the bed and the bed blew up."

"It was fitted with a bomb and as neat a wiring job to set it off as the bomb squad's ever seen. If you'd sat on the bed, on any part of it, you wouldn't be here now."

Dan grinned wryly. "Good thing I brought my bag home to unpack it, isn't it?" He winced as pain stabbed through his chest. "How bad am I?"

"Not too bad, considering. Day or two in bed and you'll be as good as new. The blast blew half your clothes off. Some flying metal caught you on the leg and in the chest. Couple of patches here and there under your pajamas, but nothing you won't outlive."

When he looked at the girl, she smiled. "It woke us up. I ran upstairs while Mom called the police, then a doctor, after I yelled you were unconscious."

Dan wiggled his fingers at Mrs. Prentice. She smiled and waved back, then began to sniffle. Dan said, "I'll pay for any damages, naturally."

"The place is insured," Thyra told him.

"Even against bombs?" he wondered.

"Well, maybe we'll have to find out about that."

"I can't stay here, taking your bed."

"Yes, you can. The doctor said you weren't to be moved for a day or two." She patted his hand again. "We're going to take real good care of you. I'm phoning the office that I'm not well. On account of the bomb, you know. So I'll play nurse, with Mom's help."

Ben lifted out a pipe and turned it over and over, staring at its polished bowl as if he'd never seen it before. Dan thought he looked more like an Indian than ever, with his color heightened to a dull bronze and his black hair shaggy and rumpled. Thyra looked at him doubtfully.

"Do you want me to go out and close the door?"

Ben smiled faintly, nodding.

When they were alone he pulled a chair beside the bed. "Anything you can tell me, Dan?"

"No more than I have. It was the same ones who tried to shoot me before. They've been after me as if they were bucking for first prize."

Ben looked thoughtful. "You had no chance to rig that bomb. Mrs. Prentice made up your room Saturday —yesterday. Aired it out, made the bed. There wasn't any bomb there then. I called the Lodge after Willie Magruder told me where you'd been the past week. I talked to Donna—nice girl, that one—and Pops."

"My God, you told Donna?"

Ben flushed and nodded. "I had to, Dan. We like our citizens alive here in Yonkers. We don't want them getting shot at or blown up. Donna said you were with her all day Saturday, most of Saturday night, and Sunday. And Thyra heard you come in last night, heard you going up the stairs."

Dan remembered the way he'd tiptoed. Damn good thing the girl had perfect hearing. Vardon spread his big hands wide apart. "You're in the clear. There wasn't time for you to have rigged the bomb. Whoever did it must have come in Sunday while the Prentices were out. Took him an hour, maybe a little more, to do the job."

Dan shivered. His mouth was dry, suddenly. For the first time since the bomb had gone off, almost in his face, he knew a real and terrible fear. Instinctively, he hunched down inside the covers.

Ben watched him. After a moment he drew out his tobacco pouch and began to fill the pipe very deliberately. "This will be in the newspapers tomorrow. I suppose the 'Herald Statesman' will play it up big. There'll be a cry for an official police investigation. Reporters will be swarming all over your garage. I've told Willie to keep his trap shut."

Dan chuckled, picturing the dour Scot being annoyed by reporters. Ben grunted, picturing his thought. "I want you to keep quiet too. Oh, not in here. Mrs. Prentice won't let anybody in. She'll keep you nice and quiet. It's afterwards I'm worried about. Your wife dying in that auto accident. The robbery at the garage. Some reporter may get smart, link them together, ask questions. Don't tell him anything, Dan. Not a thing."

"I won't."

"Me, you can talk to."

Ben leaned forward. His black eyes were hard, bright. "Go on, Dan. Tell me what you suspect."

It didn't hurt to raise his eyebrows innocently, Dan found. "Me?" he asked. "I've told you before, I don't know a thing." He wondered if Donna had told Ben about Fred Jackson and his red Triumph.

Vardon sighed, shaking his head, looking down at the pipe he had not lighted. "You still want to play it cosy?"

"Hell, Ben. Haven't we gone over this enough in the past so you'd know I don't have a clue in the world?"

"I thought you might have learned something new."

He rolled his head back and forth on the pillow. The detective sighed and got to his feet. "All right. I'll let you sleep." To his surprise, Dan found his eyelids were even heavier than they had been. He let them close.

He woke to the beat of rain against the bedroom windows and the smell of roasting lamb in the air. He lay without moving, studying the blank whiteness of the ceiling. Tiredness was an ache in every muscle, and it seemed that, outside of his eyes, he was dead.

He slept again.

Perfume. The brush of flesh across the back of a hand and the low murmur of voices. Dan looked. He saw Donna sitting in a chair close beside the bed, her head turned a little as she chatted with Thyra lounging in the doorway, a hip against the jamb. Donna was toying with his hand idly as she talked.

"Hi," he said.

The word came out as a croak, but it brought both girls to the side of the bed, Donna leaning forward in the chair, Thyra bending above her. Dan grinned and cleared his throat.

"Have I been like this very long?"

"Two days," Thyra said. "It's Wednesday."

He came up to an elbow. The weakness was gone, washed away by his long slumber. Renewed energy flooded him with his every heartbeat. It was almost as if he'd never been sick.

"I've got to get up."

Donna pushed him flat. "The doctor's due any minute. He said you'd probably wake up feeling fit after the shock wore off. Just wait until he checks you out." Then she smiled and blew him a kiss. "Hello, Dan."

"Hello, Donna."

"I'll leave you two to talk," Thyra said lightly, and moving to the door, closed it gently behind her.

Donna arched her eyebrows. "I didn't know your landlord had such an attractive daughter. Ought I be worried?"

"Thyra?" Dan asked with a queer lurching inside him. "A good kid. She has too many dates to bother about an old guy like me."

"Old guy?" Donna queried wryly. "I just hope you live to be an old guy. Oh, Dan—it must have been awful."

"Funny thing about it is, I feel fine now. It's as if it was just a bad dream. When did you get down?"

"Monday morning, first thing."

"You still at that motel?"

Her thumb indicated a cot squeezed in between the bureau and the footboards of the bed. "The Prentices insisted I stay here. I—ah—told them we hoped to get married in the fall. Was that all right?"

There was laughter in her voice and Dan grinned, clenching a fist and making a playful pass at her jaw. "You bet it was all right." Then he grew thoughtful. "I'll have to move out for a while, I guess, until they get upstairs repaired. Maybe I'll move to that motel where you're staying, or into that new motel just off Yonkers Avenue."

"The Prentices are arranging to have your apartment done over. It'll only take a week. As soon as you're on your feet, they'll have the carpenters and plasterers in."

They talked until Thyra came down the hall with the doctor.

An hour later, Dan was dressing.

The doctor had said, "It was shock, mostly. No bones broken, no internal damage. Just take it easy for a few days, no heavy work, no lifting. In a week, you'll never know you had a narrow escape. Not physically, at any rate."

Ah, but mentally? That could be another story. A man never forgets an experience like that. Especially if it was likely to happen to him again. Hell, he'd be scared to sit on a chair from now on, let alone a bed. If it happened once, it could happen again.

He winced when he saw his face in the bureau mirror. He looked like a beatnik with his beard and unkempt appearance. The first thing he had to do was make himself presentable. Then he'd take a little run up to White Plains.

There was a gleaming new sign, in red letters on a white background, announcing the Jackson Trucking Company, Inc., above the glass brick and plate-glass front of a low, modern office building just off Maple Avenue. Dan Kinnick pulled over to the curb and sat a while, just looking.

Donna was somewhere behind him, parked out of sight.

She had insisted that she follow him, promising not to show herself. There was a tacit understanding between them that his own promise not to speak to Jackson could be forgotten since the bomb incident. All Donna asked was that he be careful.

Dan got out of the car and walked across the street.

A middle-aged woman at the reception desk asked his name and gestured him to a seat. After ten minutes, the intercom buzzed. She listened a moment, then nodded Dan through an oak door.

He found himself standing in a large office fitted with a sleekly modern executive desk and swivel chair, low bookcases along two walls, and half a dozen oil paintings arranged around the gray walls. A man was sitting behind the desk, regarding him curiously.

Dan almost did not recognize him. Jackson looked slimmer and younger, for one thing; Dan supposed it

had been his hunting clothes and stubble-bearded face
that had thrown him off; it was four, five months since
he'd seen him. Now Jackson was wearing a striped tweed
and narrow tie. His face was clean-shaven and his hair
recently cut.

Dan began, "I feel pretty silly about this visit."

Jackson interrupted him, giving him a broad smile,
and coming to his feet, walked around the edge of the
desk, hand outstretched. "Not at all. I remember you
now. Indian Head Lodge back in October. I brought a
cigarette case of yours down for you. I mailed it to your
wife."

A pulse quickened in Dan's jaw. "You mailed it? She
said you brought it in person."

Jackson showed surprise. "She did? I can't understand
that." He smiled suddenly. "Unless she wanted to make
you jealous. You go home and ask her again."

"She's dead."

Jackson whistled softly, "Say, I'm sorry about that. I
didn't know."

Dan shrugged. "It doesn't make any difference. She's
dead and nobody can change it. I was passing by and
happened to think about you. I remembered I never did
get to thank you for what you did."

He had the feeling this meeting was going badly, that
Jackson was laughing at him behind the sober mask of
his face. Maybe he should have brought Thyra Prentice
along to identify him as the man who'd been seeing his
wife. But no, he didn't want to involve Thyra in his
affairs. If Jackson really were the man trying to kill
him, he wouldn't stop at getting rid of a witness against
him.

Nor could he lash out with his suspicions. How did
you accuse a man whom you'd seen only once in your
life of planting a bomb in your bed? He'd ask the police
to lock you up as a dangerous lunatic. Frustration and
helplessness boiled in Dan Kinnick.

He said lamely, angry at himself because of that weakness, "Well, I guess that's all. I just wanted to say
thanks."

Jackson nodded agreeably. "Any time, fella. You'll
always find me here." He did not offer to shake hands

again. Inwardly, Dan raged at himself for his self-consciousness. He bobbed his head and backed toward the door, fumbling blindly for the big brass knob. This man with his expensive clothes and smooth manners, framed against the background of his neat, costly office, made him feel a damned fool.

The door opened. He stepped out into the reception room, wondering what had gone wrong. There were so many things he'd meant to say, and they all remained unvoiced on the tip of his tongue. The red Triumph, and how often Jackson had come calling on Midge. The meetings he'd had with her, while Dan was working at the garage. Dan Kinnick had been the aggrieved person, yet he'd acted like a moron. Fury was a red flush on his cheeks as he moved out onto the sidewalk.

Looking neither to left nor right, he walked across the street and got into the Olds. An inner voice snarled in his mind. You stupid bastard! This was your chance and you muffed it. What excuse will you have now to see him again, face to face? His hand keyed the starter to life, pumped gas to race the motor.

He hoped Donna would have sense enough not to let herself be seen trailing him. He didn't dare risk waving her off. When he turned to scan the oncoming traffic he laid his gaze on the other cars parked on both sides of Maple Avenue. He didn't see her Comet. His hand swung the steering wheel as the Olds slid from the curb.

He would wait for Donna in her motel room.

She arrived ten minutes after him, flushed and excited. She had driven past the trucking company office, she explained, and had parked ahead of him down the block. She'd gone into a dress shop and bought a sweater and while she waited, she had stood at the store window watching the trucking concern's office front. She had seen him emerge and drive off. Right on his heels, Jackson had left the office, watched Dan drive away, then had walked off down the street. He had seemed nervous and angry.

Dan admitted to his sense of defeat.

Donna shook her head. "I think you handled it just right," she told him encouragingly, lighting a cigarette and shaking out the match. "Suppose you had lost your head and accused him of carrying on with Midge? What would you have gained? Would you expect him to admit it?"

"Well, no. I guess not."

"You saw him. I think you gave him to understand you were suspicious of him, that you didn't buy his story of being the innocent, helpful character he wants to appear. You shook him a little. I have the feeling— if he really is the person behind these attacks on you —that he'll intensify his campaign to do you in."

Watching her, Dan saw her hands were trembling, that she was fighting hysteria. He reached out, caught her wrists and drew her down on the edge of the bed beside him.

"Hey, relax. You've been a big help. This thing is starting to work out. We're beginning to pinpoint these murder attempts. At last we're getting somewhere."

She let her head rest on his shoulder when he put his arm around her, saying in a tired voice, "Dan, I hope so. But I feel this thing is too big for us to handle. Can't your detective friend do anything?"

"Maybe he is, maybe he's got a tail on us."

"We'd have noticed."

"Not necessarily. But you reminded me that I want to phone Ben, ask him to use his influence to get me a license to carry a revolver. For my own protection."

"Will he?" Donna wondered.

Ben Vardon would not, as he told Dan firmly over the motel telephone. "You think we want you staging a gun battle on the streets of Yonkers, man? God knows how many bystanders might get hurt. Just leave everything to us."

"Are you putting an around-the-clock watch on me?"

"Dan, you know I can't do that."

Anger brought a metallic taste to his tongue. "Then why the hell won't you let me protect myself?"

"What good would a gun have done you against that bomb?"

"It may not be a bomb next time," Dan growled. "Look, Ben. Try to understand what I'm saying. There's a man in White Plains, owns a trucking company. Fred Jackson. He owns a red Triumph. I think he was playing around with Midge while—all during—no, goddamit! I'm not out of my everloving mind. I got witnesses. Ah, maybe now you'll listen to me."

He talked fast, about what Thyra Prentice had told him, about meeting Fred Jackson at Indian Head Lodge, about his lost silver cigarette case, and how Jackson had returned it. His words fell over one another getting past his lips.

"Jackson and Midge were having an affair. They wanted to get me out of the way."

"Why?" Vardon asked crisply. He was all ears, now.

"How the hell should I know? I'm stating facts, not conclusions. Maybe Jackson was the only one who wanted me dead. He arranged for me to have an accident in the Buick. He sent somebody to do something to it. Midge didn't know about it and took the car instead. She got killed in my place."

"It makes sense. At least it listens well."

"Jackson still wants to kill me. But why, dammit, why?"

"You say it's Jackson. You got any proof?"

"Proof? Hell, no."

"I can't act without proof, Dan."

"All I'm asking is a gun to protect myself."

He could hear Vardon sigh. "All right. I'll take it up with the chief. If he says you get a license, you do. Fair enough?"

Dan was not satisfied, but he found himself agreeing. What other course was open, he wondered, except go down into New York City and shop around for a revolver. Pay somebody a small fortune and walk off with a .32 or a .38 weighing down a pocket. He had the feeling this might not be the smart thing to do.

He hung up and turned back to Donna.

"I'll have to give Willie a hand at the station," he said heartily. "I've stayed away long enough. I'll be working late, so don't worry."

She nodded, got to her feet and kissed him. "Be careful, Dan. Be as careful as you know how." She frowned. "In a way, I agree with Ben. Having a gun will make you reckless. You'll want to shoot it out, instead of running."

"A man gets tired running all the time."

"You know the old bromide about running away to fight another day. Just think of me, Dan. Maybe it will help."

It did help, he found, as he inserted gas hose nozzles into car tanks, and checked tires for air and motors for oil. If he stayed alive and this trouble got settled, he stood to marry Donna Morrison, come the fall. This was worthwhile waiting for, patiently and with whatever common sense he could muster.

His vacation at the Lodge had done him good. His mind was on business, and he handled himself and his tools with the dexterity of the expert he was. Business was heavy. The double column on the front page of the 'Herald Statesman' had brought him notoriety of a sort. Curiosity seekers came to fill their tanks and have a look at him.

Not until after nine o'clock did he get a chance to answer the telephone. Willie was dead beat. Dan sent him home about eight-forty-five. The telephone rang at nine sharp.

"Kinnick?" asked a muffled voice.

"Kinnick speaking. Who's this?"

"My name doesn't matter. You don't know me. It's just that I feel sorry for you. You want to know who's been taking pot shots at you, you come to the Yonkers Avenue overpass of the old New York Central's Putnam division tonight at midnight. No sooner, no later. Alone."

Excitement was a series of internal explosions making him sit up straight and listen with all the energy in his body. "Can't you tell—"

"Not over the phone. Your wire may be tapped. Tonight at midnight. If you bring the police or anyone else, you'll never learn a thing."

"All right, I'll be there."

As he put the phone back into its cradle, Dan Kinnick knew one thing. Even disguised, that voice had not belonged to Fred Jackson. It had been the voice of a woman.

CHAPTER TEN

His watch said two minutes to midnight.

Dan Kinnick stepped out of the Oldsmobile and drew a breath of cold February air. Overhead, the moon turned the snow along the slopes of Tibbett's Brook Park to molten silver. He was conscious of the increased pounding of his heart under his woolen shirt and car-coat.

A cold voice whispered in his mind, you are a fool to come here like this, offering yourself as bait to a murdering bullet. Have you no sense at all in your thick skull? He grew conscious that his hand was shaking; he balled it into a fist and hit it against the side of the car.

He had to forget his fear. He'd be no good at all to Ben Vardon, hidden somewhere here for a glimpse of this faceless someone who was out to kill him, if he let fright get the better of him. There was only one thing to do, walk like a man up the little hill and across the patch of weeds to the rusted rails of the abandoned New York Central tracks and onto the overpass above Yonkers Avenue. The tracks were rusty beneath the snow. They had not been used in a long time. The metal sides of the bridge were tall, so high they would hide him from the street.

He ran up the little slope, the abandoned overpass ahead of him, gloomy and filled with shadows, silvered by snow. His eyes went this way and that, hungering for a sight of Ben Vardon, but knowing he would be hidden too securely for chance discovery. Over the phone he'd explained about the nine o'clock phone call. Ben had been anxious for him to keep the appointment;

he'd promised to leave at once, to spend three cold hours hidden somewhere close by so he might see his informant and close in on him. Or her.

There was a good chance that whoever came to meet him was the would-be murderer. In that case, Ben would put a bullet in him before he did the same to Dan Kinnick. At least, he thought glumly, moving across the snow, that was the plan.

He walked out onto the overpass bridge.

I make a good target here, with the snow below and behind me, framing my entire body. The wind blew past him, cold and damp, making him shiver. He turned his stare along the tracks, vainly hunting the shadows for a glimpse of someone hiding there.

Dan began to walk. His footfalls sounded like echoes to the wild thudding of his heart. He went to the end of the overpass, turned and looked at the lighted windows of the big motel. Then he swung on a heel and came back.

It was fifteen minutes after midnight.

"Dan!"

The voice came out of the darkness to his right. He swung around, saw Ben Vardon moving through the snow. Relief washed over him in a warm wave.

"Nobody showed," Dan called, walking forward.

"I know. I got here about a quarter to ten and scouted the area. There wasn't anybody here then and nobody's come along since." He turned and waved an arm at the big motel on the south side of Yonkers Avenue. It loomed large in the darkness, many of its windows yellow with light. "Somebody could be in there, I suppose. Watching. Maybe they saw me, maybe they didn't."

Dan looked at the motel. "You think anybody'd risk a shot from there?"

"Not a paid killer. And nobody else in their right senses. I watched the motel while you were walking back and forth. Nobody opened a window or leaned out."

"Maybe he or she saw you and got scared."

"Maybe."

Something in the other's voice made Dan scowl. "Or maybe there wasn't anybody who called, is that what you're thinking? Goddamit, Ben, tell me the truth. Do you think I made it up?"

"No, no. I think there was a phone call."

Dan ground his teeth together so that his jaw muscles bulged. "The hell you do," he grated. "Well, screw what you think."

Almost blinded by cold fury and frustration, he began walking toward his car, parked near the lumber yard on Yonkers Avenue. He heard the detective running after him. A moment later a big hand closed on his arm, halting his stride.

"Dan, Dan," the detective chided. "Don't go away like this. I'm your friend. I believe you. Don't get the wrong idea."

Anger made a throb in his ears as a red wave washed across his eyes. He wanted nothing so much as to strike out at this big man, knocking him ass-over-heels out of his way. After a moment he realized he was being childish.

"All right, Ben. I'm sorry. I've been under a hell of a strain lately. This joker always seems to hit out at me when there aren't any witnesses around."

"He's only playing it smart. Real smart."

"Yeah. So I've got to be just a little smarter."

"Don't get any crazy notions, Dan. It's just possible that whoever set up this meeting tonight wants to learn where you're staying. Maybe he—or she—didn't have killing you in mind at all. He figured to get you here, let you stew a little, then follow you to your motel."

Dan scowled worriedly. "I never thought of that."

"Well, I did, hiding here and freezing while waiting for you to show. You go on ahead. I'll wait a while, see if anybody makes a move to go after you. That way I'll pick up anyone who does, so you know you'll be safe."

"For a little while, anyway," Dan smiled wryly.

He held out his hand. Ben caught it, gripped it. Then as if embarrassed, they looked away from one another. Kinnick muttered, "If anything comes up, I'll get in touch."

"I want you to, Dan. I honest to God do."

Vardon walked him to his car, stood there until he'd

backed around and swung out onto Yonkers Avenue. As he rounded the curve just before the Cross County overpass, Dan saw him bulking large and dark in the rearview mirror.

Back in his motel room, he took a long time to fall asleep. The phantoms of his worry were growing with every passing day. Somewhere out there beyond these motel walls was a man who wanted him dead, who was trying with every trick in the book to put him in his grave. Fred Jackson? Or some other, unknown killer? Maybe it was a madman. Or it could be a person out of Midge's past, some man or woman who fancied he or she had a grudge against him, who'd hired a trigger-man to gun him down, or kill him in any other way he could.

He lay on his back, staring at the ceiling. He turned on his side. He drew up his legs. He stretched them out. He lay on his back. He lay on his front. And still he didn't sleep. After a while he found himself listening for the telephone to ring. Then he remembered that the killer didn't know he'd moved out of the Prentice house and into this motel room until his apartment could be repaired. And Ben Vardon was making sure he—or she —wouldn't find him now.

Dan felt a little better about things. His enemy wasn't omniscient. There were limits to what he knew, what he could do. That was why the woman had phoned the garage, earlier in the night. She didn't know where he was living. Dawn was in the sky when he fell asleep.

At ten minutes past eight next morning the phone rang. Sleepily he rolled over, lifted the receiver from the cradle.

It was Donna, eager and excited. "Dan? I've just had the most wonderful idea. I'm going to play detective. Listen."

"What are you talking—detective? Now, look, honey—"

"You and I both think the man we're after is Fred Jackson. Your friend Ben Vardon can't do anything about him without some kind of proof. That's where I come in. I'm going to follow him around for the next couple of days, see where he goes, who he talks to, stuff like that."

He was sitting up in bed, faintly angry and very worried. His hand went back and forth over his crewcut. His mouth was parched, dry. His eyes seemed glued together by lack of sleep. It was hard to concentrate.

"Donna, honey. Listen to me. You can't do that. I won't let you. There's too much danger. If—"

She giggled across the wires. "I'll love it. Jackson's never seen the car I'm going to hire from one of those Hertz places. I've got a couple of different outfits."

"Oh God," he groaned. "Disguises, yet."

Her laughter came through clear and vital. It stabbed terror deep inside him. "Goddamit, Donna. I won't let you. Listen to me. You just have to listen. I'll go away with you. We'll get married right now. But—"

"I adore you when you're masterful, Dan. Honestly I do. But I've made up my mind to help, and I'm going to do what I can. I'll report back to you tonight. Call for me at eight. We'll have dinner together."

The phone went dead.

Dan sat in the rumpled bedclothes and swore. He dredged his mind for the choicest epithets he knew, remembering the oaths and blasphemies learned on street corners and in Korean foxholes. He cursed for five minutes without repeating himself. Then he gasped for breath.

He felt better, a lot better.

He was tense and nervous all day long, fighting panic at the thought of Donna getting hurt, telling himself no harm could come to her, that nobody would dare assault her in broad daylight. He argued with himself without conviction, and shook with relief when she telephoned at three minutes past six.

"No luck, Dan. See you at eight."

They came close to an open break over their cocktails at the White Turkey, where they went for dinner. Dan wanted her to drop her game. She protested it was no game to her; she was damned serious about it.

"I love you, Dan Kinnick. I won't be the first or last woman who's done a little fighting for her future husband."

"Donna, I forbid it."

"Dan, I don't care whether you do or not."

He glared at her. She smiled at him.

They finished their shrimp cocktail and roast beef in total silence. Over the dessert, Donna put her hand on his and squeezed. "Dan? Give me two days. I promise if I don't have any luck by then, I'll give it up."

"All right," he grumbled. "Seeing that I can't do anything to stop you, I might as well agree."

They went dancing at Paradise Inn.

The second day was also uneventful, though Dan felt nervousness building in him like the steady pounding of a pneumatic drill. That night he tried to dissuade her again while they were on their way to Stamford to a movie.

"One more day, Dan," she said stubbornly. "Just one."

"You haven't learned anything. It's a waste of time."

"If it is, I'm in absolutely no danger."

He found it impossible to argue that point.

On the morning of the third day, Dan knew he could never get through it. There was no use trying. Somehow, he had to stop Donna. He phoned Willie at the garage, told him not to expect him and to get one of his cronies to give him a hand, pay him a sawbuck and take an extra sawbuck for his troubles. Willie was affable and grateful for the bonus.

Dan dressed swiftly and ate breakfast in a diner two blocks from the motel. Then he went out to find Donna Morrison. He parked downstreet from the Jackson Trucking Company office and spent five nickels in parking meters and as many hours without seeing either Donna or Jackson. By midafternoon, he was pale with anger and frustration.

He drove to a Howard Johnson stand and made a lunch of two hot dogs and a tall orange drink. While he sat eating, he tried to think. It was slow going. His imagination was running wild. All he could see were mental images of Donna being slapped around by a couple of beefy men in snapdown brim hats and topcoats, while Fred Jackson lounged in an easy chair, looking on.

"I'll kill the bastard," he said out loud.

A woman customer gave him a funny look and a

clerk, scooping ice cream from a bin, turned around and stared. Dan bit into his hot dog and growled deep in his throat. This thing was really getting to him. He had to resolve it, one way or the other. He was turning into a character.

He drove to Yonkers and bothered Willie and his friend at the garage; both of whom, they informed him glumly, had been doing fine until he showed up. After an hour of looking at their faces, he drove back to White Plains.

There was still no sign of Fred Jackson.

He waited until six o'clock. When the receptionist came out wearing her hat and coat and locked the office door, he gave up. The day was over. He'd had it. Driving to the motel, he told himself Donna would greet him with a kiss and laughter. Nothing had happened to her. He was a fool to worry.

After a hot shower, he put on his best suit, a charcoal gray mohair, his best tie, and his sterling silver cuff links. He drove slowly up Central Park Avenue to her motel. He parked the car and walked to room No. Seven.

To his infinite relief, Donna opened the door.

"Hey, you're early," she said. "I said eight."

His wrist watch told him it was seven-fifteen. "I couldn't wait," he told her honestly. "I was scared witless."

"Darling," she murmured, opening the door just enough for him to slip in. There was tenderness in her dark eyes. "I haven't lipsticked yet, so you can kiss me."

She was wearing a thin shantung wrapper, a flowered print. Under it she had on stockings and a garterbelt. She was warm flesh and perfume in his arms as she opened her mouth to him, letting him squeeze her until her ribs ached.

"Worried, weren't you?" she asked mischievously when he let her go.

"Damn right I was worried. It was a fool thing to do."

"Somebody has to be on your side, Dan," she said with a catch to her voice. "I'm your team. Your only team. I wouldn't have it any other way."

"Yeah, but—"

"I was only trying to help."

Her eyes were veiled by downcast lashes. Dan had the feeling she was laughing at him. He grumbled, "Hell, I was afraid something might've happened to you. For the past three days I've been afraid."

Her lashes lifted and now he saw the mischief gleaming in her eyes. She lifted her arms so the wrapper sleeves fell back. "Dan, I've had a wonderful time. I never had so much fun. Men can be so stupid—especially men like Jackson. He was so intent on his own affairs, he never once gave any thought to the fact that somebody might be just as interested in him."

She fell onto the edge of the bed and looked up at him. Never had she looked more appealing, with the wrapper open to reveal nyloned legs and bare thighs and part of an unclad hip. Thick black hair hung down about her shoulders. Where the light penetrated the flowered print, he could see the whiteness of her breasts.

"Like what you see, Dan Kinnick?" she teased.

He flushed, then grinned. "I'm almost forgetting I'm mad at you. But seriously, honey—I hope you're all through with this private-eye career of yours."

"Mmmm, maybe I am. I learned a few things today."

"What things?"

She lifted her leg, smoothing the nylon up over her knee and thigh. "About where Jackson went and what people he saw. One place he visited, there was a Cadillac parked in the drive."

He could not breathe. "A Caddy?"

"A black Caddy. When Jackson came out of the house, a big man came with him and stood a little while on the top step talking, then went back inside the house." She nodded her head at the night table. "The little notebook, Dan. Pass it to me, please."

She opened it, gave him times and addresses.

"Hold it," he said suddenly. "What was that last one?"

"Hamilton Avenue."

His head began to pound. "In the Bayswater section? It wouldn't be number 345, would it?"

"Why, yes. Who lives there?"

"Oh, God," he whispered, feeling sick. "A Mrs. Conover. I service her car. I was at her house that night in

December when I saw the men in the Caddy that first time, when they took a shot at me. The same night I first saw Ben about it, to tell him what happened."

She stared at him. "What would she have to do with it? Dan, you never—that is, did you ever make a pass at her, get her mad or something?"

"For that you kill a guy? No, I never did. But what connection can she have with Jackson? Could she have set me up for him, calling about her battery? Brought me all the way up there knowing her friends were going to try and put a bullet in me?"

"But why, Dan—why?"

"I don't know. I don't know."

After a moment she said, "You see I was a little help, after all."

His hand fumbled across the counterpane for her fingers, squeezing them. "You were a big help, honey. A hell of a big help. But this has to be the end of it. You've got to go back to the Lodge."

"Oh, no," she protested. "I'm not leaving you down here alone. I'd just about die up there wondering if you were alive or—"

"What about your teaching career?" he asked with a smile.

"Teacher's convention," she said easily. "Two days off. I skipped it, figuring this was more important."

"All right. You've had your fun. Tomorrow you go back."

She sighed, "Dan, it's got to be settled, one way or the other. You can't go on like this." Her eyes looked worried as she studied him. "What are you going to do? If I do go back to the Lodge, what about you?"

He said heavily, "I'm thinking that I've got to get Jackson out into the open."

"How?"

"By letting him know I suspect him."

"He'll only step up his pace."

"Sure, but this time I'll be ready."

"For a shot in the back?"

"Out in the open. Some place where I stand a chance."

"Where is that?" she asked him scornfully.

"You'll see when the time comes. Now get dressed.

I'm starved. I'll take a bite out of you if you're not ready in five minutes."

"I might not mind that," she giggled.

Dan got to his feet. "I'll wait outside. It'll be safer."

"Chicken," she said, but drew the wrapper closer about her. She wanted to cry, watching him move to the door and open it. He was so damn brave, wanting to fight this thing alone, not wanting to involve her. Well, maybe she could help just by keeping him cheerful.

She dabbed perfume behind her ears and on her throat. Head tilted, she considered herself in the bureau mirror, a smile curving her mouth. Her black dress, the one with the eyelet bodice, might help tonight. She reached behind her to undo the strap of her brassiere. Maybe one way to keep him smiling was to show him a good time.

The woman phoned again next morning, a little before noon.

"I told you to come alone to the Put station. You sicced your cop friend on me. That wasn't nice, Mister Kinnick. It cost you."

"Who is this?" he snarled.

The voice in his ears was either unknown to him or cleverly muffled, maybe behind a handkerchief. He hunched forward at his garage office desk, blocking out every sense but that of hearing.

"It won't do you any good to mention names. I just wanted to let you know I feel sorry for you. You had your chance and missed it. You'll never get another."

"Tell your friend Jackson to come after me himself, next time," he said suddenly, on impulse.

There was a long pause.

Then, "I don't know any Jackson."

Was that faint alarm he heard in the faceless voice talking across the wires? Well, by God! Maybe, at last, he was getting through to them—whoever they were—and scratching the surface of the big blank wall he was up against.

"What makes you think I know a man named Jackson?"

"Just a hunch."

"I don't."

"All right, you don't."

"Maybe I'll call you again, Mister Kinnick."

The line went dead.

Exultation leaped in Dan Kinnick. Go ahead, you bitch. Run to Jackson and tell him what I said. This might bring him out in the open, face to face. His big hands balled into hard fists. What wouldn't he give to be off alone somewhere with Fred Jackson, just the two of them, ready to go at each other with bare knuckles! No guns. He wanted no killing. Fists were enough to pound the truth out of him.

"Mr. Kinnick," said a voice.

Dan looked up, startled and suddenly afraid. A man stood in the office doorway staring at him. With the daylight behind him, he was only a black silhouette. Then his eyes came to focus and he recognized Purcell, the Aetna man.

"Hello," Dan said dully. "Come on in."

Purcell nodded shortly and stepped forward. He carried his briefcase under his arm. As he sat down, he laid it flat across his thighs. His face was almost expressionless.

"We're re-opening your file," he said in his flat voice.

"Why?" Dan snapped.

"I understand someone's been trying to kill you. Why, Kinnick? Unless this would-be killer of yours fell in love with your wife and knows or guesses that you tumbled onto it and—in a fit of jealous hate—caused your wife's death in that auto accident."

Dan said slowly, "Well, that's one way to look at it. Only trouble with your theory is, I never knew about my wife's lover until after Midge was dead and buried. So I couldn't kill her for something I didn't know about, now could I?"

"Not if you're telling the truth. No. Still, since a murderer can't receive insurance policy proceeds for the death of a person he kills, the company is naturally interested in your innocence or guilt. You've received forty thousand dollars from Aetna for your wife's death. If you killed her, then that money isn't rightfully yours."

"I haven't touched a penny of it," Dan snapped, "if that's any consolation to you."

Purcell smiled gently. "I'm only re-opening the case, not instituting an action to recover the money. For me to do that, you'd have to be adjudged guilty of murdering your wife, Kinnick—and Ben Vardon assures me you're innocent. He makes out such a good case in your favor, I'm of half a mind to leave the file closed. But I like to play it safe. I'll re-open the file and just let it lie, waiting."

"What does that mean?"

"You're free to come and go. Aetna will wait on the district attorney. If he takes no action against you, now or hereafter, Aetna will consider the case closed. We've got to protect ourselves, naturally. To be quite honest, we'd have liked to get out a court order impounding the money for a reasonable time, just to make certain you didn't run off with it—or possibly to restrain you from leaving the jurisdiction of the Court—but our legal department isn't sure they could make it stick."

Coldness drove deep inside Dan Kinnick. To have come this far, then to be brought up short by a court order—No. Fate couldn't be that cruel.

He had to be free to egg Jackson into taking another step against him, but at a time when he would be ready to fight back. If he were restrained in his freedom of movement, even for a short time, he'd lose the initiative. His entire success might depend on what happened in the next couple of days, before Jackson had a chance to think things out. He wondered if his thoughts showed on his face.

Purcell stood up, tucking his briefcase under his arm. "I just thought I'd let you know, and advise you to watch your step."

"Maybe you're hoping I'll do something which will let you act. Is that it? Give me enough rope to hang myself? You bastard. You and your court orders. All I have to do is make one funny move—anything at all—and you'll pounce."

Purcell shrugged and went out into the waning daylight. Dan sat crouched over his desk, thinking about Donna Morrison. Marry her and Aetna would pick him

up so fast, his head would spin. They would have a motive
for the murder then. He felt a scream coming into his
throat, compounded by the frustration and fury that was
eating inside him. He bit down hard on it.

He had to act fast. Time was running out on him.

He meant to marry Donna. Not all the insurance
companies in the world could stop him. But he had to
be a free man, first. He had to find out who was after
him, who wanted him out of the way and why.

If he was wrong about Jackson, he was dead.

Really dead.

Unable to sit still, he got out of his chair and walked
around the little office, past the piled cans of motor oil,
the racked tires, the pyramid of new batteries. He studied the calendar girl hanging on the wall beside the desk,
his desk pen set and cigarette lighter.

He walked around the room again.

Now he was looking at the Auto-Lite batteries. That
made him remember Mrs. Conover on Hamilton Avenue and the night he'd installed an Auto-Lite in her car.
He needed to see that woman very badly. But what the
hell excuse could he give for barging in on her unan-
nounced? It had to be a good one.

Or did it? After all, if Jackson was as guilty as he
hoped, she might be in this up to her ears. From what
Donna had said, she knew Jackson. Suppose she had fingered him for those killers in the Cadillac last December?
Certainly, she wanted no trouble from the police.

He reached for the telephone.

After a moment he heard her voice.

"Dan Kinnick, Mrs. Conover. You know, the garage
man."

"Oh, Dan. Yes, of course. What is it?"

"I was wondering if you could help me."

"Why, I—I suppose so. If I can, that is." Wariness
was in her voice, but that might be natural.

"You remember the night I brought the battery to
you? Back in December? Well, on my way home, a man
took a shot at me. Yes, that's right. With a revolver. He
tried to kill me."

"Oh, that's terrible. Awful. Bu-but what can I do?"

The quiver was there, now. He could catch it. Maybe

the rich bitch was a little worried. He had to be careful. One slip-up and he was finished. He needed time to think.

"Might I come over this evening for a little talk? I don't want to blab my suspicions over the phone. For all I know, my line may be tapped. The police were called in, you understand."

"Tonight? Why, I'm not doing anything, going anywhere. I guess you could come over, yes."

"Thank you, Mrs. Conover. Shall I make it around nine?"

"Nine will be perfect."

"Good-by, Mrs. Conover. I'll see you later."

"Yes, of course," she replied thoughtfully.

Dan let the phone slip from his fingers. If his suspicions were correct, she'd be busting a fingernail dialing Fred Jackson to let him know that he'd phoned. However, he didn't think she'd stand for any murder attempt on him in her own home. She might be willing to finger him, but she'd want the killing done somewhere else, so as not to involve her.

Dan dressed in his motel room as if he were going on a date. He made a presentable figure of a man, he thought, staring at his mirrored reflection. Wide across the shoulders, not much to his middle—the way he worked, he never had any trouble with weight control—and tall enough. He guessed he'd pass muster. His face was a little craggy, but passably good-looking. And his crewcut hair was all his own.

He grinned at himself. "I'm no Tab Hunter, but I'll get by." He wondered vaguely about Mrs. Conover's love life. Could be she was hungry, being a widow—unless Jackson was getting some of her—and perhaps ripe for a healthy pass.

He ate a steak at Howard Johnson's, then gunned the Olds for the Bayswater Knoll section. There was a hunting rifle on the front seat of the car, tucked close below the sliding seat. It was a criminal offense to carry a rifle in Westchester County, but he'd risk that trouble if the Caddy came by with its beefy marksman. His palms sweated. God! Just once to be able to draw a bead on that car, its right rear tire, for instance, or its gas tank. A brass-jacketed .30-08 would go into all that high-octane fuel with the destructive power of an ICBM.

He pulled into the drive and parked.

CHAPTER ELEVEN

The house was lighted only by a few lamps in the living room. He thought as he rang the doorbell that maybe he was a damn fool to be coming here like this. He felt reasonably certain Mrs. Conover would want no killing in her own house, but he could not be positive, of course. There was always the chance—

Sweat stood on his forehead. His hand shook.

Dan removed his hat and used his other hand to run a handkerchief over his forehead. He'd made his play. It was swim or sink. He only wished he'd told Ben Vardon where he was going.

The door opened and Mrs. Conover was smiling at him.

"Come in, Dan," she said softly and stood aside.

She wore tight lounging pajamas of some black clinging stuff that showed every line of her body. Pearl ropes hung about her throat, gleaming white and lucent against the black pajama bodice where it hugged her full breasts. Dan was agreeably surprised. She had an exciting body. Maybe it wouldn't be as easy as he'd thought to make a pass at her and keep a cool head.

Mrs. Conover walked ahead of him into her living room, and as he followed, Dan found himself staring at the gently mounded buttocks which trembled so delightfully at her every stride. She must have painted that black stuff on, it was so tight. He followed it down each leg to the bare ankles and the high-heeled shoes.

"What'll you have?" she asked, pausing at the wall bar.

"Rye, thanks. With rocks."

"I used to like rye, but my late husband changed me into a Scotch drinker. Now I prefer it."

"Tastes like medicine to me," Dan commented honestly.

She laughed and held out his drink to him. Her eyes were feverishly bright, and he had the feeling that she'd belted down a couple of those Scotches before he rang the doorbell.

He sat on the big sofa while she eased ice cubes into her old-fashioned glass. His eyes turned slowly from the recessed blue niches with their ceramic vases on display to the huge abstract colorscape on the panelled wall behind the combination fireplace and bookshelves. The room was tastefully furnished. Dan Kinnick had been in enough homes like this to know excellent decor when he saw one. He wondered where a widow got the money to keep up a place like this.

She stood at the bar sipping her drink, studying him with bright eyes. After a moment she put the drink between both palms and held it pressed to her middle as she asked, "Now then, what's this all about?"

He spoke of the night in December when the first shot had been taken at him, along Colonial Road not too far from her house.

"As if they knew I were coming here and waited for me out of sight, then followed me. I suppose it's silly. I told myself it was, right after. But I went to see a detective friend of mine, Ben Vardon, after I got to thinking about it. I figured it wasn't the first time somebody had tried to get rid of me."

He went on to tell about the car accident which had cost Midge her life. As he talked, Mrs. Conover moved away from the wall bar and walked up and down thoughtfully, with her head bent. Dan wondered if she realized she was giving him a damn good look at her body.

And he looked, even as he talked. He guessed he'd have to be a little more than human not to look, not to be aware of the excitement curling like wisps of electric smoke at his loins. Her big breasts rode easily without a brassiere to hold them in, ripely nodding, and he was fascinated by the gentle shifting of her hips. She was soft white warmth under those black pajamas. Any man would have itched to peel them off.

He made himself sit still and manufacture words.

After a little while he discovered that he was making no sense, so he shut up. Mrs. Conover was right in front of him, smiling down at him. Her glass was empty. So was his, he saw as she bent to reach for it. He let her take it.

"So you think I may be connected with these murder attempts?" she asked as she crossed to the bar.

"Hold on. I never said that."

She slid ice cubes into his glass, turning to smile at him. "No, but you've been thinking it. Come on, now. Admit it. Otherwise you wouldn't be here."

"I was just wondering if you'd heard anything from your neighbors—you know how nosy neighbors can be —about two men in a big Cadillac waiting in the shadows that night somewhere down the block."

Her head tilted. "Mmmm, no. Can't say I have."

"Well then, maybe I ought to be running."

"Oh, not so soon," she told him, bringing him his drink, sitting beside him, curving one leg up under the other, leaning a shoulder into the sofa backrest. "You only just got here. I'm glad you're here, Dan. I've been lonely lately."

He looked down into his rye, mumbling, "I've been a little lonely myself." His mental fingers crossed as he thought of Donna Morrison. The thought touched his mind that maybe they were both lying.

"I know," she murmured, understandingly, brushing his wrist with her warm fingers. "Your wife." Somehow she'd come closer on the cushions. Her knee touched his thigh. The curling smoke spirals in his loins grew thicker, heavier. "But surely, you must suspect *some-body* of trying to kill you? Have you been a naughty boy, playing games with some rich lady customer and her hubby found out?"

"Nothing like that," he laughed shortly. "And I don't owe anyone. No gambling debts to welsh on, no old feuds, no fights. Nothing. Period."

She pursed her lips. "Hmmm, that doesn't sound very promising."

"Which is why I'm here, clutching at straws."

Her nose wrinkled at him mischievously. "You haven't been doing much clutching that I can see."

It was an engraved invitation. Dan hesitated only a fraction of a second before putting a big hand on her thigh. Each of them was playing a game, probing for information. If he read this woman correctly, she would bust a gut to let Fred Jackson know what she learned here, this night. And if she did that, she would be playing into Dan Kinnick's hands: for then he'd be morally certain that it was Jackson who was on his back.

But why?

His hand moved up her soft thigh to her hip, gently squeezing. He could see the excitement flare in her brilliant black eyes, their lids faintly dusted with green tinting. She wriggled closer, putting her fingertips at the back of his head, running them up and down. Awareness of her womanhood tingled down his spine.

"Much better," she whispered, and sipped from her glass.

Dan had to keep this on an even keel. He said slowly, "I know I have a hell of a nerve barging in on you like this. But I've been going quietly nuts trying to dope it out all by myself."

This might turn any suspicion away from Donna, he told himself, in case Jackson had spotted her tailing him and began getting ideas. He watched his hand moving over her rounded hip, fondling the warmth and softness of her flesh through the black pajama trousers.

"There's no need to fight it by yourself," she whispered, caressing his throat lazily with long red fingernails. "I've had my eye on you a long time, Dan." She smiled lazily at his sudden start. "A couple of times I came close to calling you up, inviting you over. In one way, I'm sorry I never did. In another—well, maybe it's better this way, when I can help you. It makes a woman feel good, Dan, when a man turns to her."

"I wish you could help me."

"The least I can do is listen. You can talk as freely as you like. If you're in some trouble, it'll be a secret between us. And maybe all you need is a woman's viewpoint."

The pitch was coming. Mrs. Conover murmured, "There are some things you don't want detectives to know. Me, I'm not a detective."

She was a woman, and a damned attractive one. She was so close now that it was a struggle not to pull out all the stops and yank her in against him. As if she sensed his hesitation, she moved so that one unbound breast nudged his upper arm. Glancing sideways, he found his gaze magnetized by the low cut of the tight pajama jacket and the full white swells of her breasts bulging upward into the vee.

"I just have one slim lead, but—"

"What is the lead, Dan?"

"Ah, hell. I can't drag you into this."

"Please, Dan. I want to help all I can."

She was making it convincing all right, so much so that a stab of guilt went into him. Suppose he had her figured all wrong? He rolled away and got to his feet, shaking his head.

"No, Mrs. Conover. I can't let you take the risk."

She came off the sofa after him, catching his arm, swinging him around and plastering her front up against him, breathing fitfully as she grasped his shoulders and held him in surprisingly strong fingers. He gave her credit. She was an actress, all right. Any poor joe who'd come to see her as unsuspecting as Dan Kinnick pretended to be, would have been taken in.

His hands touched her sides, moved down onto her hips. Staring up into his eyes, she argued in a fierce, hard whisper, "Goddamit, Dan. What do I have to do to convince you I mean what I say? Take you upstairs to bed? Is that the proof you want?"

"No," he protested. "I don't—"

"I want to. I want to so damn much. I meant it when I said I'd had my eye on you. Tonight when you phoned I thought, this is it. Tonight begins a new life for me. The only thing is—the first time we're meeting like this, I'd rather we didn't bed down. I don't want you to think me any pushover. I haven't had a man since my last husband died. I'm choosey, Dan. Just any man won't do me. I want somebody who'll set me on fire. As you will. You see, I'm being honest with you.

Maybe too honest. But I want you to be just as honest with me."

Of course you do, you bitch. You want me to come right out and tell you I think Fred Jackson is the man who was trying to kill me all the time he was laying my wife. A real gold-plated bastard.

"How can I refuse you anything?" he asked out loud. Let her think she was a suburban Mata Hari, if she wanted.

Her hands slipped up from his shoulders to lock around his neck. Her soft body mashed into him, wriggled for a better fit, then began its subtle movements. And her ripe red mouth opened to his kiss. Dan felt as if he were plummeting down into moist warmth. For a moment he swung weightless in time. The floor disappeared beneath his feet and only his lips and his hands clinging to this woman held him anchored to the world.

Then everything came back into three-dimensional solidity. "God," he whispered, and looked at Mrs. Conover with new eyes.

"You see?" she asked softly.

He had been too long without a woman. Only that one night with Thyra Prentice since Midge had died. He was ripe for somebody like Nell Conover.

She spoke again. "You see what I can mean to you, Dan? I knew it would be this way between us."

"I don't know what to say."

"Then don't say anything. Let me do the talking. We can have so much, you and I. So very much. I've had three husbands. Two of them I divorced. The last one died. I don't think I want to marry again, Dan. At least, not just yet. But I'm lonely. I need affection, a lot of affection. I think I can get that from you."

He kissed her again, unable to stop himself, then let her palms push him away. "Not too much of that, lover. Mamma is human. Tomorrow night we can have our party."

"I'll have trouble getting to sleep," he grinned.

"Ah, won't I? But in this one thing, humor me."

"Sure. But tomorrow'll pass damn slowly."

She rested her cheek on his chest. "Dan?"

"Mmmmm?"

"This trouble you're in. Is it because of some woman?"

"No. I honestly don't know any reason for it."

"You said you had a slim lead."

Dan drew a deep breath. He had to make this look as if her kisses and her perfumed flesh were drawing this information from him almost reluctantly. "A man named Jackson. He has an office in White Plains. I think he's the one behind it all."

His hands on her back grew aware of her stiffening muscles. As if she knew she had betrayed herself, she made them relax to their former softness. "What makes you pick him out?"

"I met him up at Indian Head Lodge last October. Between then and the time my wife went over that hill in the car, he got to know her pretty well. Too well."

The muscles were rigid under his hands again. In a jealous spasm? She whispered, "How well is too well?"

"He was having her," he said bluntly, and told her what Thyra Prentice had said. If Nell Conover was Jackson's woman, she'd do a burn over this. When she called him later, if she did, she'd make the phone lines sizzle.

"It doesn't add up. Just because he was making love to your wife before she got killed in that auto accident doesn't give him a motive for wanting you dead."

"I know that. There has to be another reason, but I can't think of any."

"He may not be the one at all."

"I know that, too. Call it a hunch, if you like. A feeling. But ever since I met him, the trouble started. My wife getting killed in that auto accident could have been a mistake. Jackson may have been trying to kill me, not Midge."

"This is all pretty wild, you realize."

"I told you I was clutching at straws."

She moved out of his arms, went for their glasses and filled them. He came to stand beside her at the wall bar, sipping the rye. She was flushed, excited; but this might be because of their kisses.

"What are you going to do about him?"

"Nothing. I can't prove anything. It's all conjecture."

"The police won't help you?"

"I have no proof. Neither of the men in the Cadillac was Jackson. I didn't get too good a look at them, but I'd swear to that."

"What I can't understand is, why he should want you dead. If he had a yen for—for your wife, there's always the divorce court."

"I told myself that. And there isn't any other reason. I met Jackson in October. He was a stranger to me. I never saw him before and to my knowledge, he never had seen me."

"Dan, you must be on the wrong track."

"Maybe I am. I said it was only a slim lead. Built up out of thoughts, of knowing he was having my wife when I wasn't around. No more."

She held her glass so tightly her fingers looked bloodless. "It must be hell on you, living the way you are, and not knowing when a bullet will come out of the night."

"And not being able to hit back. I think that's the worst part, being so defenceless."

"Why not go away? With me?"

He chuckled, "I'd like that a lot. But what good would it do? When we came back, my friends would come gunning for me again. Or put another bomb on my bed. How could I enjoy myself, knowing I had to come back to that?"

She bit her lower lip. "Of course. I'm sorry."

"No, don't be sorry. I've been thinking of running away from it, I'll admit. Of selling my gas station and moving somewhere else where they couldn't find me."

Her plucked eyebrows lifted. "And?"

"I haven't made up my mind. I suppose I ought to go somewhere quiet where I can think about it, weigh the pros and cons."

Now he was ready to make his own pitch, to tell Mrs. Conover what he wanted her to relay on to Fred Jackson when and if she called him.

"I think that's a wonderful idea. Some place quiet."

"Indian Head Lodge, maybe. Nothing relaxes me like a tramp through the woods this time of year. The hunting season's over. I wouldn't even have to carry a rifle. I'd just put my hands in my pockets and walk."

Nell Conover caught his hand. "Oh, Dan—yes! The woods. Lonely, quiet, with nobody around. You can get things all straight in your mind. About selling the gas station, about getting out of Yonkers." She added suddenly, "And about us, too."

About us, in a pig's eye. She was seeing an imaginary Dan Kinnick walking alone and unarmed through the woods around Mount Arrowhead, a ripe target for a man with a hunting rifle in his hands. The man holding the rifle was Fred Jackson.

Or was he doing her an injustice?

There was only one way to find out: by going to the Lodge and walking alone in the woods, offering himself as a target.

A chill ran down his back.

He took a long swallow of the rye to restore his courage, then put his empty glass down on the wall bartop. "Time I was running. If I stay any longer, I won't be able to run."

She had retired inside a shell, he saw. The Nell Conover who had kissed him was gone, leaving this woman who was anxious to be alone, to make her phone call. She put her glass beside his, nodding.

"Maybe you'd better, Dan."

An imp of deviltry made him ask, "What about tomorrow night? You said I should come over, that we'd have ourselves a party."

She grew confused. Fear glinted in the eyes she lifted to his face. "Do you think you should? With—that is, everything considered?"

He wanted to laugh, but did not dare. She had to continue to believe him the nincompoop he was making himself out to be. He hoped that his face mirrored the disappointment he wanted to make her think he was feeling.

"Maybe you're right."

"I think you ought to get away."

"The Lodge, you mean?"

She nodded, touching his hand with hers. "Think it all out, Dan. Then come back and tell me what you've decided."

"If you want me to."

His words made her remember her role. She came into his arms, lifting her mouth for his kiss. The spark was out of her, now, though; to Dan the caress was cold, calculated.

She walked to the door with him. As she put a hand on the knob, she turned to him. "When are you leaving, Dan?"

"Oh, some time soon."

She frowned. "The sooner the better, you know. What I mean is, the quicker you make up your mind, the sooner you'll be safe."

"What do you think I ought to do?"

Let her put the finger on him, set the time and place. In that way she could call Jackson's shot. She seemed to be considering. Finally she wondered, "Why wait? Why not go tomorrow?"

"Tomorrow it is, then."

"Phone me before you go?"

He nodded, feeling her hand on his upper arm beginning to push him through the door. What a simpleton she must think him! He felt vaguely insulted, then reasoned that he wasn't playing games. This was a deadly business between them, with his life at stake.

The cool night folded around him as he stepped out onto the front porch. The door closed behind him. The lock snicked into place.

Dan sighed. If he was right in his suspicions of Nell Conover, she was hotfooting it right now to her telephone, dialing Fred Jackson, telling him where he could find that stupid fool, Dan Kinnick, all alone and without a gun in his hands, any time after tomorrow evening.

He walked down the path and onto the gravelled drive. From here he could see into the living room. A shadow touched the window and Dan bent his head to enter his car. Nell Conover was taking no chances. She wanted him out of the way before she called Jackson.

His foot started the engine purring to life. Head out the window, he backed onto Hamilton Avenue. A moment only, he paused, to swing his loaded rifle off the floor and onto the seat. He didn't think Jackson would

risk a try for him tonight, not with his having come
to visit Mrs. Conover, but he would be prepared.

He drove to his motel room in perfect safety.

Nobody even followed him.

CHAPTER TWELVE

The Luger automatic lay on his motel room night table, its eight-inch barrel giving it a lopsided look. But the M1917 Borchardt was a model of balance and accuracy. Handcrafted, it had been manufactured for German machine gunners during World War I. Every part of it was clean, brightly polished. Dan Kinnick had taken it apart and put it together again. It was like new.

The magazine which fitted to the base of its frame held 32 rounds. When used with an attachable stock, the Luger made a perfect rifle. And Dan Kinnick had the stock. All afternoon long on a worktable in the garage he had been cutting and shaping the wood and attaching leather straps.

He had bought the Luger in a pawnshop on Third Avenue in New York City, in a store where his ten twenty-dollar bills talked louder than his lack of a pistol permit. The clerk had seemed utterly indifferent to the fact, asking no questions.

"The man who pawned it hasn't come back in eleven years," the clerk had volunteered. "It's a damn fine gun, but it's got too long a barrel."

"The long barrel adds to its accuracy."

The clerk stared at him. "Kind of hand guns customers want nowadays—at least, the kind of customers we usually see for guns—is something small and deadly at close range. Not this thing. You could shoot deer with it."

"Yes," said Dan softly. "I know."

Or a man.

The Luger had an accurate range of eighty to a hundred yards. Its bullet would travel close to twelve hundred yards, but Dan had no such distance in mind. The way he figured it, fifty to seventy yards would be about right.

The attachable stock would let him aim it like a rifle. He was more familiar with a rifle than a revolver or automatic. The stock had another advantage, too. He could hide it under his jacket, the way he could hide the Luger in his belt. From a distance he would appear unarmed. And if Fred Jackson refused to take a shot at an unarmed man, he had him tabbed all wrong.

Only one thing was left to be done.

He had to call Nell Conover, let her know he was going up to the Lodge first thing in the morning. She would give Jackson plenty of notice.

Then it would be kill or be killed.

She must have been waiting beside the telephone. It rang once; then her voice was at his ear, faintly excited as she said hello.

"Nell? Dan Kinnick here. I promised I'd call, let you know when I'm leaving. Tomorrow first thing. About eight. I'll eat breakfast on the road."

"I'm glad, Dan."

"When I get back, shall I call you?"

"Of course. I want you to. Then we'll have our party. Just you and me, the two of us. A whole weekend together."

You heartless bitch. You think you're talking to a dead man, holding out a promise you never mean to keep. I should have put the blocks to you last night when I had the chance. Give you something to remember me by.

Only the thought of Donna Morrison had stopped him. Even while he'd been kissing Nell Conover and holding her soft buttocks, he'd hated her. Maybe it had been the hate that had triggered his desire for her body.

He said, "I don't know how much clear thinking I'll get done with that weekend in the back of my mind."

"Dan, you have to," she scolded. "I want you to go for nice, long walks. Really long ones. Get away from everything."

Far enough into those woods, the sound of a rifle

would be muffled, hidden from curious ears. His lips twisted grimly.

"All right, if you say so. I'll think it all out, whether it'd be better for me to sell the station and buy a new one five hundred or a thousand miles away—or keep on playing tag with somebody's bullets."

"Yes, Dan. Please do. For me."

He let his voice grow diffident. "Well, I guess—I don't have anything else to say right now. I—I just wanted you to know."

"I'm glad you did, Dan. Now—bye-bye."

The phone clicked in his ear.

He waited ten minutes, slowly smoking an Old Gold. Then he dialed Nell Conover a second time.

He got a busy signal.

All he had to do now was write a letter to Ben Vardon, telling him where he was going and what he intended to do. Ben would get the letter tomorrow morning. By then he would be walking the woods around Mount Arrowhead.

Fred Jackson would be walking those same woods, hunting him.

Too late then for Ben Vardon to refuse to give him a gun or to let him risk his neck finding out the truth about Fred Jackson. He was not asking permission now. He was just telling the detective how he was going to solve his case.

Or die in the attempt.

There was a hint of snow in the gray sky as he urged the Olds at a steady sixty miles an hour along the Thruway. Snow might ruin his entire plan. It was scarcely likely that Jackson would go tramping through the woods with a rifle under his arm knowing that the white snow would frame his body to the sharp eyes of an expert huntsman like Dan Kinnick.

No, Jackson would want brown boles behind which to hide while he squeezed off his shot—and dry twigs underfoot along the forest path, to give warning of Dan's approach. All the odds had to be in his favor, even to the fact that Kinnick would be unarmed.

Well, it would appear that he was unarmed.

The Luger would be in his belt and its homemade stock hanging on a hook sewn to the inside of his Mackinaw. The magazine would be in a Mackinaw pocket. The fun would go out of it for Fred Jackson when Dan Kinnick began shooting back at him.

It was high time Dan Kinnick began having fun.

He drove easily, without worry, filled with a sense of timelessness, as if this journey on which he was engaged had been written in some eternal scroll half a billion years ago. He did not know how his journey would turn out, or even if he would be alive to make a return trip. The only thing that mattered was that he was on his way to come face to face with his destiny.

The gray clouds rolled away while he was between the Sloatsburg service area and the Kingston turn-off, and the sun broke through. By early afternoon the day was bright and sunny and, for February, quite warm. He took it as an omen.

God knows he needed omens, and good luck charms, and anything else with which to bolster his confidence. He could understand now how the ancients never made a serious move without consulting an oracle. He wished there was an oracle he could consult. An Empire State Building sibyl, mouthing ambiguities. He supposed that over the centuries, man came to depend less on fortune-tellers because he learned to depend on himself and his own resources.

Like Dan Kinnick, with a Luger and a homemade stock.

He parked close to the front porch of the Lodge's main house, unlocked his trunk and carted his new valise—the old one had gone up in the bed explosion—into the huge sitting room. Emotion held him in its grip a moment as his gaze brushed across the room. The deerheads hanging on the long wall above the fieldstone fireplace: how long ago was it since he'd first laid eyes on them? Twelve years? Fifteen? He'd been fourteen at the time, he remembered. Must be more than sixteen, seventeen years now. So long? More than half of his life.

In a way it was fitting that he had come here to fight

out this crisis, here where he first started to live as an individual. Any other place would have no meaning for him. In these woods around Indian Head Lodge he had become a person with likes and dislikes, with a sense of belonging, of being an integral part of the life around him. Until then he had been a boy, molding his character in a classroom. Here, he had become a man.

Now he would defend his rights as a man.

The right to life, to the liberty of walking where he would without a fear of death always crawling in his guts, the right to the pursuit of his future happiness with Donna Morrison. He thought he might be getting corny, but he didn't give a damn. When you were face to face with living or dying, things took on a different meaning.

"Hey, Pops," he yelled.

The back door opened and closed. Johnny Anson came stamping into the living room, pausing to stare in disbelief, then holding out his hand and grinning.

"Danny boy, it's good to see you."

"I'll be staying a few days, Johnny. I had such a good time before, I decided to come back. Give me a room. I want to wash up, then eat."

"Donna mightn't be back 'til late. She said she'd stay in town to see a movie."

"I'll get a good night's sleep, then. I want to be up early and walking in the woods."

The older man smiled mischievously. "Shall I tell her you're here?"

"Not if you can help it. I want to surprise her."

Johnny went behind the registration desk, fumbled for a key, then tossed it through the air. Dan caught it, pocketed it, lifted his bags. He would take his shower, get dressed in slacks and flannel shirt, maybe take a short stroll before supper around the Lodge grounds.

He woke next morning at six, discovering through the bedroom windows that the day was gray and overcast. Dan was strangely pleased. Weather like this would tempt Fred Jackson out of White Plains. Visibility in the Mount Arrowhead woods would be poor, but good enough for a man to stand hidden behind a bole and put a lead pellet into his victim. Dan wanted to give him every opportunity. Traffic would be light with the threat of snow in the sky. There'd be fewer cars to buck along the Thruway, fewer eyes to see the killer as he came and went.

Yes, he rather thought Jackson would take the bait.

And he had to play target for the man, get him out of his shell into some overt act that would be proof positive that Jackson was the one who wanted him dead. He dressed slowly, without emotion. His mind had accepted this fact for such a long time that he had no feeling about it. It was time for the little drama to end, in the only way Dan Kinnick might have a fighting chance for his life.

When he was dressed he put the Luger into the pocket of his red Mackinaw and put the homemade stock into its sleeve. He carried the Mackinaw downstairs and hung it on the hall rack.

Johnny Anson had told Pops about him. Donna's father came to share a coffee and cigarette with him as the time crawled on toward eight. Pops seemed flustered.

"Aren't you going to tell Donna you're here?"

"Later. First thing I want to do is get out into those woods. I want to walk and walk and walk. Nothing else. I've got a monkey on my back and I've got to get rid of it the only way I can."

Pops was too smart to ask questions. He finished his coffee, snubbed out his cigarette, then rose from the table. "Got to help Johnny out back, Dan. Good luck, boy. See you at lunch." He hesitated, then added, "Or supper."

"Lunch or supper. Right, Pops."

He lingered over his cigarette another five minutes, then went out into the hall, transferred the Luger from his Mackinaw pocket to his belt, and slipped into the heavy woolen jacket. He removed the plywood stock from the sleeve and hung it on safety pins inside the Mackinaw. He tested the hang of the hunting jacket. It fitted well enough and was only mildly uncomfortable. Even up close, he saw in the hall mirror, his appearance would not arouse suspicion.

He lit another cigarette on the front porch of the main building, staring across the way at the big barn where Donna was probably dressing right now to attend her classes. Emotion gripped him. If everything went right today, he wouldn't have to hide from her like this any more.

Dan gave his head a little shake. He couldn't afford to think about Donna. Not now. Not this morning.

He angled his walk away from the Lodge, across a corner of the parking lot, along the path which led up over the hill where he'd first seen Fred Jackson with a Winchester in his hands. Buck fever had held him in its grip. He had been so excited, he'd flung the rifle from him in among the ironweeds and gayfeathers.

Funny how things worked out. Now he was hunting for Fred Jackson to give him a chance to kill him. Just as Jackson had been trying to kill him ever since he'd met him. But why? Why? Not just because of Midge. He could not believe that, yet there seemed to be no other answer.

He came to the top of the hill. He made a good target standing here against the sky and his skin crawled. But no, it would be too early for Jackson to drive up from White Plains, searching for him.

Or—would it?

Jackson might have left the same time he did, or soon after. Nell Conover would have phoned him as soon as he'd hung up on her—he recalled the busy signal when he'd called her back—to tell him Dan Kinnick was on his way. Jackson might have packed his gun and climbed into his car within half an hour after ringing off. Maybe he'd been all ready to go, just waiting for her call.

He would know about that, soon enough.

His gaze touched Feather Hill and the Knoll, names he and Donna had given to various parts of this landscape years ago. They used to make a game of it. What were some of the other names? There'd been a Pirates' Roost, though he'd forgotten where it was, and Gold Hill, Lilac Lane, Cowbell Path.

Stop a bit. Lilac Lane?

What did he know about Lilac Lane? It had been mentioned recently, quite recently. Oh, yes. They'd found that dead man there, a little to one side of the old path where wild lilacs sometimes grew. By craning his neck, he could make out a part of the lane from the top of the hill.

Dan shook his head. He'd never get anywhere mooning like this. It was dangerous, too. He had to be cold, hard, not soft and sentimental today. Fred Jackson, if he came, would be cold, merciless. He would lift his rifle and squeeze its trigger and kill Daniel Philip Kinnick if he could, if Dan Kinnick let him.

He went down the far side of the slope toward the woods. He walked slowly, steadily, fighting the surge of panic that made sweatbeads erupt on his forehead. A man was in those woods, about to kill him. He had to let himself be seen, had to make of himself a living target. Jackson must shoot first. Dan had to be sure before he fired back at him, and that meant he must give the other man first shot.

Walking in the open like this, through the field of meadow grass, he made *too* good a target. But he had to walk through the meadow to get in among the trees. And he had to go slowly, carelessly, as if he really were an unarmed man without a suspicion in the world that he was moving to his death.

The trees were nearer. He fought the impulse to run to them. Gently, as if he walked on eggs, he lifted each hunting boot and brought it down easily. The trees moved nearer. He was under them. He slipped between the boles of a maple and a yellow birch, taking off his red cap and wiping his wet forehead with a handkerchief.

For the moment he was safe.

To Dan Kinnick these woods were as familiar as the streets of Yonkers. In a sense he was on his own home grounds. If a man had to fight for his life, the advantage went to the one who had the choice of the battleground, all other things being equal. This was his battleground, these woods. Here he would make his fight.

He slipped between the trees and walked.

He walked a long time, until noon and after.

As he moved through the woods, he began to lay his traps. Here between two dogwood boles he tied a length of rope, smeared with dirt until its discoloration blended with the rotting leaves underfoot. A little further on he rigged a stretch of very dry leaves, the driest he could find. Anyone walking over them along the well-defined trail would sound like a charging animal.

None of his snares were intended to do more than alert him to Jackson's presence. No man could be taken as might an animal, at least not in the simple traps he only had time to set. Here he placed a long stick on which he balanced a rotting log. Its fall, as the stick was kicked, would tell him where Jackson walked. The stick was cleverly hidden by a small pile of leaves. There he put a big rock in the middle of the trail over which Jackson would have to step onto thin, dry twigs which would crack under his weight. He was trapping for sound, not for a prisoner.

Mostly he used the dirt-smeared ropes, stretched between tree trunks and knotted tightly. If he could make Jackson fall, he'd have him at his mercy.

He worked until the sweat ran off him.

And nothing happened.

There was no gunshot, no sudden explosion of sound. Only the eternal quiet of the woods, with the February wind stroking the treetops, moving them a little so that the dry, empty branches could rub together, make that hollow sound. The music of the wild places during the winter months. And a rabbit scampering across the dry leaves and pine needles, off to one side.

Dan wanted to laugh at himself.

He was so goddam smart. He had it all figured out, the part Nell Conover played, the fact that Fred Jackson wanted him dead and would leap at this chance to kill him. Well, he was all wrong. It wasn't that way at all.

Jackson was probably back in White Plains, minding his own business. He had no interest in whether a man named Dan Kinnick was alive or dead. It was somebody else who'd been trying to kill him for the past few months.

But who? Who?

A glance at his watch showed the time to be ten minutes past one o'clock. He'd been tramping these forest paths and laying his traps for more than five hours. His legs were tired and he was a long way from the Lodge. Time to retrace his steps.

It had taken him five hours to get this far, walking

slowly. He'd have to step up to his pace if he wanted to get back to the main house before dark. He began to hurry.

He was coming out of a juniper thicket when something rammed his shoulder and yanked him backward. He fell into the junipers, gasping for breath, half stunned. As his wits returned to him, he rolled over and over toward the thick bole of a·big hickory tree.

A sound ripped the air apart. He knew it was the echo of a high-powered hunting rifle: maybe a Winchester, maybe a Savage. He lifted a hand and put it to his left shoulder. There was a hole in the red wool.

Shock had numbed his nervous system, but he knew he'd been hit, that the bullet, to judge by the hole in his Mackinaw, had caught him high up in the shoulder, probably missing the shoulderblade, but ripping through his trapezius muscles. He put a hand behind him, and relief made him lightheaded. There was a hole back there, too. At least the bullet had gone through and out of him.

"Hey, you—Kinnick."

The voice floated at him from the west. Dan got to his knees, cursing his carelessness. He'd made up his mind too soon. He'd forgotten to be careful, intent only on hurrying back to the Lodge before dark. He wondered if Jackson had figured on that fact. Was he so smart? Despair touched him a moment. Despite all his planning, he had walked into a bullet like a nincompoop. Shock still ran in him like a flood at spate.

"Kinnick, can you hear me?"

He recognized the voice. "I hear you. Are you crazy, man?"

"Not crazy. Smart. I've got you right where I want you. Helpless with a bullet in you. Without a gun."

"You're Jackson, aren't you? Fred Jackson?"

Jackson did not reply. While he waited, heart pounding savagely, Dan fumbled the Luger out of his pocket, grimacing. The shock was wearing off now and the pain was beginning. He moved his left hand before it got too bad, yanking at the plywood stock, tearing the wool of the Mackinaw when the safety pins held. With trembling fingers he fitted the stock to the barrel, tightening the butt screws with his penknife.

From time to time, he lifted his head, listening.

Jackson was close by in these woods and edging closer for a better shot. He would know about where Kinnick had fallen and would be coming for him, rifle up and ready to fire.

Sweat stood out on his forehead as he cursed the rashness that had made him come here alone, offering himself as a target. All his clever plans to trap this killer had blown up in his face. He wished now he'd brought Ben Vardon with him instead of merely writing him a letter.

The Luger was ready, though. The stock fitted perfectly, holding firm under his testing hands. Now if he could circle around and come up behind the other man—

He began to crawl slowly and with patience between the tree boles like an Indian. Time was an eternity of pine needles and bark and underbrush scraping at his clothes. The Luger was in his right hand. He had pushed his useless left arm between the buttons of his red hunting jacket to form a sling until he needed it to support the hand gun.

He was nearer to the trail but not near enough. Jackson had fired from behind the big rock pile off to one side, as best he could judge. Another hundred yards of crawling and—

Shock held him rigid.

Jackson was twenty yards away and moving toward him, rifle at the ready, eyes hunting the underbrush. Dan swung the Luger up and tried to yank his left arm free from his improvised sling. He could not budge it. His right hand had to catch it, draw it from between the Mackinaw buttons.

The arm was useless. He could never use it to steady the Luger, hold it motionless while he aimed and squeezed off a shot. He was as helpless as if he really were unarmed, the way Jackson thought.

But he had to shoot, if only to warn Jackson away.

Another ten feet and the man would fall right over him. Jackson couldn't miss at such close range.

Blindly he fired, swinging the gun up with his right arm, pressing the plywood stock against his side. He heard Jackson shout in amazement, then in sharp pain.

Dan grinned with bloodless lips. Sheer luck had let him score a flesh wound, maybe, something painful to judge by the vicious way Jackson was swearing; but nothing serious, nothing that would slow the man in any way.

He had to come up with a plan of action, or he was a dead boy. Dan waited, holding his breath. The shock of the recoil had started his wound bleeding more freely. He could feel the wetness on his shoulder, running down his chest.

He could bleed to death out in these woods unless he got help. And he could never do that with Jackson waiting to stop his bleeding forever. He was getting weaker. He had to get a doctor at that shoulder soon. No doctor would come walking through the woods. Dan had to go and get him. And he was pinned down by the threat of Jackson's rifle.

Dan cursed softly, in utter helplessness. His entire left side felt paralyzed now. He reached out with his right hand and caught the root of the hickory tree where he lay, pulling himself forward. He had to get at Jackson. Somehow, in some way, he had to hit back at him.

A bullet exploded in the tree bole about three inches above his fingers, showering him with shredded bark and splinters. It had been close. All he needed was a busted right hand to go with his helpless left. Then Jackson could pump a .270 between his eyes without anybody stopping him.

He groaned.

This time the bullet was less than an inch from his head. If his right cheek had not been scraping the ground as he moved, his brains would be splattered all over the hickory roots. He wanted to close his eyes and sleep. He had to fight against dizziness.

He stared at his hand. It was shaking uncontrollably. His brain had no power over it or over the muscles of his body. The Luger was quivering in his hand like a live thing. The pain and the shock and the loss of blood was getting through to him. He was ready to black out.

All Jackson had to do was walk over and shoot him.

He fainted before he could be afraid.

CHAPTER THIRTEEN

He swam out of that blurring weakness, lifting his head and looking around him, suddenly aware that only seconds had gone by. Jackson was still hidden in the underbrush. Dan moved the fingers of his right hand, getting a firmer grip on the Luger.

He felt stronger. The wound had stopped bleeding, was caked with dry blood. His left arm was numb, but the pain had lessened.

Or maybe he'd been out longer than he'd thought. Jackson might have realized he'd keeled over and was coming for him by a roundabout way. Cautiously he turned his head, staring this way and that, but not seeing or hearing the other man. Where could he be? In front of him? Behind him? Off to one side? He had to know. His life depended on the knowledge.

He let go of the Luger, reached for a pebble.

He threw it and heard the faint snick it made hitting a tree bole. It was the only sound in the woods. If Jackson was anywhere about, he was keeping very quiet. Too quiet.

He reached out, caught hold of a tree root, dragging himself forward, his useless left arm thrust into his belt to clamp it to his side. His eyes raked the woods. Fifty yards away, between those two dogwood trees lining the trail he had tied one of his dirt-smeared ropes. If he could lure Jackson out from behind those rocks—

He crawled faster. When he was hidden by a bole, he lurched to his feet and ran, making no attempt to hide his blundering progress. Any moment now he expected to hear the explosive report of the Winchester, maybe

139

even feel a bullet ramming into his back. He glanced behind him.

He saw the rifle poking between two rocks. The barrel was steady, unmoving. He fell just as the rifle spat red flame at him. Visibility was close to zero this far in among the trees. Jackson had taken a long time to aim. He could not know whether his shot had hit home or not.

Dan screeched as he went sideways.

He lay a moment, then rose and went forward, but now he walked carefully, planting his feet flat, with knees bent, as the Indians had travelled when these forests had been their home. He made no more noise than a shadow.

The strung rope was behind him, taut between the tree boles.

Dan lay down, holding his breath. He had a chance if he could get the other man to come stalking him, too busy with looking for Dan Kinnick to notice the hidden rope across his path. But the Luger was too clumsy to handle with the stock on it. So the stock had to come off, to turn it back into a hand gun again.

His good hand fought the screws holding the stock to the automatic. Get the stock off and he wouldn't need his left arm. This close he ought to be able to aim the Luger with reasonable accuracy, even though he wasn't too familiar with hand guns. Maybe the threat of the gun would be enough if Jackson took a hard tumble.

He worked as quickly as he could, but it was a slow process. He lost a frame screw and had to fumble around in the pine needles for it before he could get it back into place and ram the magazine home.

Then he reached for a rock and put it close beside his right hand. He was hoping Jackson would think him dead, drilled through by his last shot. For half an hour he lay there, listening to Jackson calling his name every so often. It seemed he scarcely breathed.

There was movement along the trail. Jackson lifted into view, rifle ready to be snapped to his shoulder. "Kinnick?" he called.

He waited two minutes, then came forward. He moved slowly, alertly. Dan knew he was no stranger to danger, this man. His eyes were never still. He walked with a light step and was prepared at every moment to fall, belly down, in cover.

Dan waited, hidden by a berry-bush thicket.

Jackson was close to the hidden rope now, less than ten feet away. Just a few more yards and he would be able to see between the berry branches, see the man waiting for him with an automatic in his hand.

Dan put the Luger on the forest floor, lifted upward and hurled the rock he had placed within a hand's reach. The stone made a curving arc through the air, thudded into dry leaves and tree roots a hundred feet to the right. He had timed his throw just right.

Jackson whirled toward the sound, turning and taking an instinctive backward step.

His heel hit the rope. His feet went out from under him.

Dan came to his feet, staggering because his left arm clamped in his belt threw him off balance. The Luger was firm in his right hand, though. He growled, "Freeze, Jackson. Freeze right as you are. Now take your hand away from the rifle. Easy does it. There."

Jackson lay propped on an elbow, glaring at him. "You bastard," he said softly, and the hate was alive in his eyes.

"Sure, I know. I feel the same about you. Now get on your feet and let's get the show on the road." His glance touched the Winchester which had been jarred from Jackson's hand by his fall and was lying in the bushes. "I'll come back for it, or send someone. I can't carry it and I won't let you. Start walking, man."

Police Chief Andrews stood over him in the Lodge kitchen while Doc Broome bandaged his shoulder. Ben Vardon—who had sirened a path to the Lodge as soon as he opened his morning mail—was framed in the hall doorway looking more like an Indian than ever, though Dan believed he saw new respect for him in his eyes. Donna sat on the edge of a chair, hands clasped, eyes enormous in her white face. Johnny Anson and Pops were making drinks at the counter.

"Tell me that again, chief," Dan said to Andrews.

"You solved my case for me. The dead man we found in the woods last time you were up, remember? His name was Max Trubo. He was Jackson's partner. Jackson killed him last October. He'd just shot him when you came walking up to him. What you thought was buck fever was sheer funk. Jackson thought you'd seen him kill him."

Ben Vardon stirred in the kitchen doorway, "Right after that, those attacks on you began. Jackson was trying to get you out of the way. He thought you were playing a cat and mouse game, setting up a try for blackmail. He took your silver cigarette case—"

"The one I gave him," Donna said softly.

"—to Midge. According to his story—we had a transcript made and he signed it—he stopped off in New Paltz to telephone Midge, telling her he saw you kissing Donna here at the Lodge. Then he went to see her next day. He played up to her in the hope of learning what you knew. At the same time, he made plans to kill you.

"He had a man who used to be in the stolen car racket break into your garage and insert old, worn brake hoses in the Buick. He figured sooner or later you'd have an accident, and if that didn't finish you off, he'd do the job while you were laid up, with Midge's help. Midge was pretty well under his thumb by that time. He even had pictures taken of her in bed with him to hold over her head if she balked. When she was killed, that plan went down the drain.

"The same man who replaced the brake hoses rigged the bomb in your bed. The goons in the black Caddy were trigger men he knew in the old days when he and Trubo had been members of the same mob.

"Jackson wanted respectability. He met Nell Conover, fell for her, got her to promise to marry him when he had some standing in the community. Until then, he and Trubo used the trucking layout as a blind to explain their income from monies they had stashed away from their days in the rackets.

"Jackson borrowed money from the firm, Trubo's money. He knew Max would kill him if he learned what he'd been doing. So Jackson killed him first. Only you saw him do it. Or he thought you did.

"By this time, Jackson had his hooks in the Conover

dame. She called up your garage at his say-so, gave you her business. She fingered you that night in December when you went to install a battery and got yourself shot at. She also phoned you the night we went to the old Putnam overpass, when nobody showed up. Used a stocking over her mouth to disguise her voice."

Dan interrupted, "What about that night, Ben? Did Jackson say what he intended to do?"

The big detective shrugged. "Jackson said his men were watching us from a motel room. They saw me and chickened out. They would have shot you down if I hadn't been there, I guess. Maybe I should have thought of the motel—but hell! I was half-convinced you were seeing things at that point."

"Yeah," said Dan wryly. "I know."

Vardon scowled. "While we're on the subject, why'n hell didn't you let me know ahead of time you were coming up to the Lodge to act as bait for Jackson?"

Kinnick grinned, "Honestly, Ben—would you have let me? I bought a Luger in the city. You'd already told me not to. But I had to do it. I was damn tired of playing target for those killers."

Ben said thoughtfully, "Yeah, maybe you were right at that. As a cop, I couldn't let you risk your neck, but maybe it was the only way to bring Jackson out into the open—and still give you a fighting chance to save yourself."

Donna exclaimed reproachfully, "Just the same, you could have told us."

Dan grinned at her. "You wouldn't have let me go into those woods any more than Ben would. Besides, I didn't want anybody doing my job. It had come down to a man to man proposition between Jackson and me. I felt I owed it to myself to fight back."

Chief Andrews muttered, "I'll have to get your statement about what happened down on paper, the sooner the better. Jackson's behind bars, but the D.A.'ll want more than that, especially since Vardon here and I have ordered the arrest of Mrs. Conover."

Dan looked at the Yonkers detective. "She did what I thought she'd do, then? Rang up Jackson and let him know I was coming up here?"

"Just as soon as you left her house," Ben nodded.

Dan said to the police chief, "All right. Tonight after dinner. Donna will drive me into town. I'll give you your statement then."

"Good enough. I'll have a shorthand man ready to take it down." Andrews looked around the kitchen, nodding to each of them. "That ought to round it off. Good-by for now then." He smiled down at Dan and winked an eye. "And once again, thanks for solving my mystery for me."

He went out and closed the door behind him. Pops brought a drink to Dan, then to Ben Vardon. The doctor stepped back, studying the sling.

"Feel okay?" Broome asked.

Dan nodded and sipped the powerful highball. The liquor sent warmth flooding through him. Donna was on her feet, standing close and staring down at him with a feverish light in her eyes. Doc glanced at her, smiled faintly, then turned away to snap shut his black bag. Pops and Johnny walked with him to the front door.

Ben Vardon cleared his throat and came forward, offering his hand. "Got to be running, Dan. I'm glad everything turned out the way it did."

His handclasp was firm, strong.

Then he was going after the others, leaving him alone with Donna. The girl bent and caught his cheeks between her soft palms. There were tears in her eyes. Her red mouth lowered to his lips and Dan felt himself sinking into moist warmth with a wild, tumultuous excitement.

He wanted to laugh, to shout, as he put his good arm around Donna and brought her down on his thighs. He was alive for the first time in months, really alive with his blood pounding and his brain singing in a drunken elation.

Alive! No longer—as good as dead.

THE END